A gorgeous and meticulously-researched historical fiction examining a young woman's struggle to escape unexpected poverty and find autonomy and purpose in early New England.

Read *Pauper Auction* for the history of small town New Hampshire at the beginning of the 1800s. Or read it for the compelling story of Margery Turner, a heartbroken young widow who must navigate the patriarchal society of her times. The cards are stacked heavily and (to our modern way of thinking) unfairly against her. Mary Kronenwetter writes with a clear-eyed precision that deftly and gracefully shapes a story that is both true to its era and relevant here and now. Human nature doesn't change. Prejudice persists. As does hate. As does cruelty. This is a remarkable novel — historically detailed, full of heart, and shocking in the brutality it reveals. Yet there is courage, too. And kindness. And ascendancy.

~ Rebecca Rule
Author, *Moved and Seconded* & *The Best Revenge*
Host, PBS series *New Hampshire Authors* & *Our Hometown*

Kronenwetter's impressive debut follows the uncompromising lives of a destitute widow, a disabled child, and a Native American stonemason. With portentous forecasts from the *Farmer's Almanac* in the chapter headings, the domestic narrative paints a convincing day-to-day picture of early America, immersing readers into the stark realities of farm life and meeting halls. Fans of historical fiction ought to take a look.

~ *Publisher's Weekly*

While *Pauper Auction* starkly reveals the ways in which New England towns in the New Nation period addressed the needs of the destitute within their communities, it also spotlights less often heard stories - those so often hidden stories of women, children, and those with stigmatized sexual orientation. This novel is neither a traditional history nor a traditional love story, yet it subtly provides rich cultural and historical details while also probing the many faces in which love manifests itself and families form. Additionally, *Pauper Auction* rejects the notion that there were no Abenaki, the Indigenous people of New Hampshire, actually living in New Hampshire after the American Revolution by including an Abenaki character in an essential supporting role. *Pauper Auction* presents a refreshingly honest, richly detailed, compelling story.

~ Anne Jennison
Northeast Woodlands Traditional Native American
Storyteller and Historian

This historical novel set in our nation's early years drew me in with compelling characters and detailed descriptions of how Granite Staters lived in post-Revolutionary War New Hampshire.

~ Laura Knoy
Author & Host of NHPR's *The Exchange*

PAUPER AUCTION

Mary
Kronenwetter

Stone Fence Press

Stone Fence Press
PO Box 1337
Grantham, NH 03753
www.marykronenwetter.com

Publisher's Note: This is a work of fiction. Names, characters, places, and incidents are a product of the author's imagination. Locales and public names are sometimes used for atmospheric purposes.
Any resemblance to actual people, living or dead, or to businesses, companies, events, institutions, or locales is completely coincidental.

<u>Book Layout</u>
Lighthouse Rocket Design, Mike Leister
& Stone Fence Press

<u>Cover Design</u>
Lighthouse Rocket Design, Mike Leister

<u>Cover Image</u>
Bed Rug, 1801, Esther Packard, American (1733-1812)
Courtesy of the Collections of Historic Deerfield
Photograph by Penny Leveritt
Mother with Son (partial), 1799, John Brewster Jr.
Courtesy of the Palmer Museum of Art

Pauper Auction/ Mary Kronenwetter -- 1st ed.
Library of Congress Control Number: 2021923317

ISBN 979-8-9852609-8-4 paperback
ISBN 979-8-9852609-7-7 hardcover
ISBN 979-8-9852609-6-0 audiobook
ISBN 979-8-9852609-9-1 ebook

To my beloved husband, John.

*Thank you for tending to our 21st century lives
while I walked in the past.*

Mankind are always seeking after happiness in some way or another.

~ Dudley Leavitt

The New Hampshire, Maine and Vermont Almanac
for the Year of our Lord 1805

Containing more Astronomical Calculations than any Almanac
of the size hitherto published in New England. With a variety of
such matters and things as well, it is hoped, be useful and
entertaining to the Reader.

Calculated for the Meridian of Gilmanton, N.H.
Lat: 43 °28' North. Long. 70° 54' West.

CONTENTS

THORNEBORO TOWN MEETING
& PAUPER AUCTION
MARCH 1805

Notice of Warrant
Freeholders and other inhabitants of the Parish of Thorneboro.
Who are by law given vote in parish affairs. You are duly notified and
warned to meet at the meetinghouse for town meeting on Tuesday the 12th of
March in the year of our Lord 1805 at ten of the clock before noon.

A stench of unwashed, damp woolens emanated from bodies packed into the meetinghouse. Belatedly, Widow Margery Turner began breathing through her mouth as her stomach roiled. She would have no call for her mouth to speak this day. Prior to the meeting, she had been instructed by Moderator Asa Judson to sit in attendance for the entirety of the day. In no uncertain terms, she had been commanded to remain silent, even on the article regarding the oversight of the poor and her own future. This was the last order of business to be considered before calling for adjournment of the annual town meeting.

Thorneboro was a rural New Hampshire hill town with stone-seeded fields and granite-faced farmers. Few houses in Thorneboro were attired in a coat of paint, but the meetinghouse was a brilliant white-robed beacon of the small town's aspirations to godliness and democracy. Today, however, it was wreathed in grey mist. Sitting on a rise in the center of town, it hosted the daylong Congregational Sabbath services, and civic events such as the annual town meeting.

There remained lingering animosity and discontent among some of the townspeople over the placement of the meetinghouse. While it was geographically in the town center, those on the hill-studded north side of town had a considerably more difficult journey without the fine road enjoyed by the south side of town. Before taxes were raised to build a meetinghouse, town meeting had been held in Gabriel Allen's tavern. Such a setting, where the men could drink spirits and argue all day, had been far more boisterous and contentious, and more than once a debate devolved into physical altercation.

Today, its bell rang to call the men to town meeting as it had rung to call the residents to mourn the passing of the town blacksmith, Nathaniel Turner, not so long ago. Throughout New England, town meeting was held on the second Tuesday of March. In larger towns, the meeting might run multiple days, but in Thorneboro, they finished business in one day.

The tradition of conducting town meeting in March matched the agrarian calendar and fell during the fallow period when farmers would not be planting or harvesting. A time when the long winter tapered into damp muddy days before finally yielding to an ethereal and fleeting spring. Roads were becoming passable, and all but the most reclusive of town members yearned for companionship other than their families and hired help.

The Thorneboro Meetinghouse wore three doors and a pitched roof. A grandly-columned and pedimented front door graced the south-facing side of the building and welcomed the minister, his family, and honored guests. Modestly-framed side doors admitted entrance on the east for townswomen, and on the west for townsmen. Multipaned windows illuminated the shared sacred and secular space. The townspeople were proud of these windows, ignoring the ironic fact that they had been imported from England. The clear glass windows were a symbol of the prosperity and civility of their community. Unlike the grand cathedrals of ancestral Europe, a New England meetinghouse was starkly beautiful despite eschewing religious iconography such as stained glass, statue, and cross.

Margery Turner's downcast eyes examined a small, darkened hole in the pine floorboard where a square-headed nail had previously resided. Nathaniel's nail. He would never make another nail, horseshoe, axe, or door hinge for the residents of Thorneboro. Today, the fiscally-responsible town Selectmen, the "Town Fathers," and specifically, the Overseers of the Poor, would be deciding which Thorneboro resident would take on responsibility for the newly widowed woman, aged but 27 years. She was one of the paupers being bid out at auction today.

Being put up for *vendue* was the opposite of a livestock auction. Rather than bidders winning by offering the highest price, bidders for paupers came away successful by offering the lowest price they were willing to accept from the town to provide necessities to sustain the town's poor under their beneficent roofs.

Thorneboro residents complained vociferously about paying taxes for poor relief while they simultaneously lauded themselves for their Christian compassion. Some of the town poor were offered aid and allowed to remain in their homes. Those who no longer had roofs over their heads were taken in by a responsible, tax-paying town resident who would be reimbursed by the town. The able-bodied paupers taken in would be expected to undertake work to ensure that their Christian sponsor would not only cover the cost of their food, shelter, and clothing through town funds, but also make a profit from their labor.

Margery was one of the unfortunates who required placement in a home. A bride brought to Thorneboro, and not a resident by birth, she supposed she should be grateful that she had not been warned out of town, as was any unfortunate but unknown needy soul who attempted to tarry within town borders.

From her seat, Margery had a clear view of the pulpit used for Sunday morning worship. The wooden edifice rose and hung in space facing out over the pews, under a sounding board to project the minister's lengthy orations on the nature of good and evil. An arched pulpit window behind him provided light for his notes. First floor pews were family-owned. The high-sided boxes owned by the town's prosperous families could hide a sleeping child, a coal foot-warmer, or even a warm dog to lie across one's feet during endless, cold meetings. Despite its grandeur, the building was unheated due to the ever-present fear of fire.

Balconies housed single men and women, hired hands, apprentices, and those not able to afford a pew. The east gallery was designated for females and the west gallery for males. At the end of the west balcony sat a small enclosed area called the slave pew. The town's population had included a half-dozen slaves in the past. After the War for Independence, the town was home to one free black family. Prince and Evelyn Lewis managed their own small farm with the help of their four children.

Margery recalled observing an encounter between Evelyn Lewis and Shopmistress Stanton at the General Store. Mrs. Lewis had come in to trade honey from the skeps she tended. With pursed lips, Mistress Stanton had ostentatiously wiped the spotless jars, her own hands, and the counter with a cloth as she transferred vessels from the counter to the shelf behind her. Mrs. Lewis had stood straight and proud against the insult. The Lewis family had been members of the Society of Friends, more commonly known as Quakers. Recently, the Lewis family had joined the Quaker migration to eastern Ohio, where almost a thousand families had fled the religious persecution experienced in New England.

The slave pew today was designated as the assigned seating for those paupers being bid out. It was here that Margery now sat. Although she had been attempting to ignore the fact that she was not the only resident of the stall, Margery's eyes strayed to the man sitting a few feet from her. She caught the eye of her fellow "unfortunate." They nodded without exchanging a word, recognizing each other as one does in a small town. Benjamin Meakin was red-eyed and emanated a rank stink indicating the previous night's — and perhaps this morning's —overconsumption of cider or rum.

There were a number of categories of worthy and unworthy poor. Each year, town records documented the name, age, and cause of pauperism for each recipient of aid. Causes of pauperism included infirmity of body or mind, old age, misfortune of parents, intemperance, intoxication or abandonment of husband, or illegitimacy. Insanity was a broad category variously titled delirium, idiocy, or *non-compos mentis*. This gentleman fell into the intemperance category.

Margery turned her eyes back to gaze out the window. The wavy glass blurred the view. Although she could not see her husband's grave in the cemetery next to the meetinghouse, she felt its presence, his presence. *Help me face this day, Nathaniel, my beloved.* She offered up her plea for the strength to bear the feelings of indignity, shame, and powerlessness that washed over her.

"Gentlemen," began Moderator Judson. Indeed, there were no women in attendance except for Margery. "I call this town meeting to order." She guessed that Judson, like so many men, was in love with the sound of his own voice. His inflated chest was harnessed within a too-snug waistcoat secured with hard-working pewter buttons. "We have a duty, under the eyes of God, to make decisions that will lead this town on a path of peace and prosperity this coming year and this is a duty we take most sincerely to heart. We begin with reports from the year past and elections of town officers."

For the next few hours, winter-pale men stood and detailed the state of the town fences, roads, and walls, as well as the destructive antics of deer, escaped swine, and drunken boys. For a small town, there was rather a plentitude of offices and officials. One office at a time, reports were submitted, men were nominated, ballots cast, results announced, officials sworn in. Positions included selectmen, poundkeeper, auditor, fence viewer, field driver, hogs reeve, sealer of weights and measures, surveyor, and tythingman. There were almost more official positions than men. The men who wore the cleanest of clothes and boots, who lived in town, who had traded tricorns for the newly fashionable top hats, often took more than one title.

A scuffling sound pulled Margery's attention to her right. A bearded young man in ragged clothes had snuck in as the men argued about responsibility for a washed-out road. He placed a young child on the bench, prying her tenacious fingers from his coat sleeve. Her gown was worn and had been let down a number of times. Her ash blonde hair was unevenly braided, surely done by her own small hands. Her slate-blue eyes were awash with tears. The man kneeled in front of the child and whispered, "My sweet girl, you are going to go to a home where there will be plenty to eat and a hearth to warm yourself. Be a good girl and be as helpful as you can be to those who take you in. Always remember I love you. I pray I will return for you soon."

The man gently laid a crutch and cloth bag next to the softly-sobbing child. Margery noted that the girl's left foot was unnaturally twisted. A club foot, the unfortunate thing. As if being a poor girl child was not enough of a cross to bear. The man strode resolutely away as Margery turned her head to follow his progress. He descended the stairs, stiff-shouldered and without a backwards glance.

The village of Thorneboro sheltered less than 250 souls. There were no strangers and no secrets. Margery knew this miserable waif, if not by name then by sad story. The young man was her father, Rufus Bishop. His wife and the child's mother, Verity, had recently died of childbed fever, a few days after giving birth to their second child. The infant had been born blue and cold, never to open his eyes in this world.

The Bishop homestead was a few miles from the village center, still far from being cleared enough to make a profitable farm. The young man, a fourth son, had moved to this northern town with his new wife. They had been lured by the siren song of land to call their own, only to have been thrown upon a rocky shore. They had been tricked into a patch of land that offered up more glacier-scoured stone than crops. The dream of a prosperous farm and a house full of healthy and straight-limbed children lay buried near that homestead in a small casket that held both the mother and babe in her cold arms. Verity's earlier children who had not survived lay nearby.

As Margery turned back to the girl, she could feel the vibration of quivering terror in the silent child. Margery knew she should comfort the child, but felt a paralysis of terror and shame at her own predicament. She could do no more than pat the child's hands as she attempted to turn her attention back to the proceedings.

The man sharing their bench sat forward to get a better look at the little girl, whose eyes returned over and over to the stairs her father had descended, as if expecting him to change his mind and return. He reached into his pocket and took out an apple. It sported a few desiccated wrinkles, but had obviously been carefully stored in a cellar barrel since its harvest last fall. He held out the pippin to Margery and pointed to the girl. Margery offered a strained smile as she took the fruit from his grubby palm. She tried to wipe the apple unobtrusively on her skirts before passing it along to the child. Meakin caught her movement and smiled wryly into his beard. Margery handed the apple to the child, who took it without making eye contact and perhaps whispered the tiniest, "Thank you."

The morning progressed: approving the minister's salary, debating whether another school was needed for the northern section of town, setting a bounty on wolves, and other articles representing such interests and needs of the town. Upon the bell toll of one o'clock, the Moderator intoned, "Having finished the business of electing officers and other articles of importance, I propose we adjourn to Allen's to partake of the supper the womenfolk have set out." He directed, "We shall adjourn for one hour. Please limit your consumption of Allen's fine spirits so we may keep this meeting civil."

Those in the balcony, including the disheveled man who sat alongside her in their compartment, had already begun their exodus down the stairs and out the side door before the Moderator had finished his pronouncement, much to his visible consternation. Those in their bought and furnished pews on the main floor, and within direct sight of the table of selectmen, had to wait until the Moderator finished his instructions, and so were slower to exit towards the welcome respite of the tavern.

Margery remained in her seat until the men had cleared out of the building. She was of a firm mind that she would wait in the meetinghouse until the proceedings resumed. Then she looked down at the silent and shivering child sitting next to her and waivered, "Well, little one, we should probably find you some dinner." She helped the small and unresponsive girl to stand with her crutch, and they slowly made their way out of the meetinghouse and towards the icy warmth of the boisterous tavern.

Allen's Tavern was a scant yet sodden walk from the meetinghouse. From the open door, the aroma of pork, baked beans, alcohol, and wood smoke greeted guests. An open hearth with generations of cooking grease seeped into the stone underneath beckoned with the promise of warmth. The wide pine floorboards were sanded and strewn with rushes. The ceiling was low and smoke-blackened beams spanned the room. Sheep tallow candles in tin-mirrored sconces were lit against the gloom.

Some townsmen walked a straight line towards the aromatic victuals being served. Others veered towards the tavern keeper, who had raised the spiked bars on the caged enclosure from which he sold mugs of ale, hard cider, apple brandy, flip, or rum.

Tavernkeeper Allen greeted the men by name, many of whom spent more than they could afford in time and coin in his public house. George Eaton, the town's recently reelected tythingman, had no cause to censure the tavern's business today. Come Sunday, the Sabbath, his eagle eye would ensure that no liquor passed the lips of the townsmen, at least in public, as he enforced piety to the best of his ability on his fellow residents. "Come Eaton," the proprietor urged, "join us for a drink. This one day a year. It's on the house." Tavernkeeper Allen never passed up an opportunity to tease the thin-lipped and thin-skinned man. Eaton offered no response but a disapproving snort and turned his attention to his plate, while the men grinned at his expense. Brave, as most men are, when in company.

This year, Margery had not baked a skillet gingerbread cake for the annual town meeting dinner as she had done when Nathaniel was alive. Women she had known since her arrival in town five years prior now averted their eyes from her and turned to speak animatedly to whoever happened to be standing to their right or left. The young widow and the child remained in the corner, the child sitting on the straw-covered floor, until all residents had taken their plates. Only then did Margery approach the long table and help herself to the pork, beans, and some crumbed remnant of dried apple and vinegar pies. She did not smile or speak to the women, refusing to assuage their discomfort over her predicament or dignify their relief that they did not stand in her shoes.

The women's attention, although titillated over Margery's appearance, was drawn primarily to Samuell Wheeler, standing a head over most of the men, broad of chest, with auburn hair and amber eyes. He wore a deep moss-colored waistcoat with an ivory linen shirt. A black cravat encircled his neck. Although he wore the old-fashioned wool felt tricorn hat, this did no harm to his most agreeable appearance. He stood silent while the men rehashed the morning meeting and worked the room for votes on upcoming articles.

Samuell did not meet the gaze of any of the womenfolk, perhaps therefore avoiding a petty grievance between lifelong girlfriends. Margery followed the women's eyes and observed his aloof manner as well as the manners of the rest of the townsmen, wondering whose roof she would be sleeping under this night. She and the child ate quickly and departed to return to the empty meetinghouse, to the relief of many.

After an hour of eating, drinking, and catching up with neighbors, Moderator Judson announced that it was time to reconvene in the meetinghouse. A murmur of displeasure arose as the townsmen looked through the open door. The inhospitable weather had waited patiently for them to complete their repast. The men trudged back through icy muck to fulfill their civic commitment and have their voices heard and votes counted.

After the pews were once again filled and selectmen and assorted officials settled in chairs facing the town residents, Moderator Judson cleared his phlegmy throat and called for order. The next item on the docket for the afternoon session was an article presenting the petition signed by six farming families requesting the extension of road up through the hills on the north side of town and the call to collect money for supplies and labor. The auditor informed the attendees that he calculated that the project would increase their tax payments by one cent per acre for the next four years. After acrimonious arguing back and forth, the article, on recommendation of the selectmen, was voted down. The residents of the north side of town grumbled or shouted their displeasure at the decision according to their temperaments. Support of the minister was a far milder discussion. The salary and firewood allotment was voted at the same rate as the previous year.

Finally, Moderator Judson spoke the words that froze Margery's blood. He began, "We turn our attention to the 16th and final article of today's warrant, 'For the town to consider and act in the best way to Support the Poor of the Town.'" The town fathers were ready to bid off this year's paupers. "Good people of Thorneboro," he continued, "it is our civic and Christian responsibility to provide for the care of our town's unfortunates. As Proverbs 19:17 verily declare, 'Whoever is kind to the poor lends to the lord, and he will reward them for what they have done.'" The townsmen grudgingly intoned their "Amen." The Moderator concluded his introduction with, "I turn to our Overseer of the Poor, Jonah Fletcher, to provide a report and lead today's pauper auction."

A stout, flint-eyed man with a relatively-clean vest and greasy forelock stood up and surveyed the crowd. "Neighbors and townsmen," he declared, "the Office of the Overseer of the Poor has been diligent in tracing the census of our town and identifying those worthy and unworthy of receipt of precious town funds. In the Year of Our Lord 1805, I submit the following report and recommendations and present the residents to be put up for this year's pauper auction."

Fletcher paused to refill his puffed-out chest. He went on, "Firstly, in the last town meeting the Selectmen saw fit to sign an order to warn and give notice unto a transient woman and daughter lately come to this town with the intent to abide therein though not having obtained the Town's consent. They were kin to none, and had not funds for land, supplies, or taxes. A warrant ordering them to depart the town within fourteen days was issued. The woman and child departed for parts unknown and have not returned." A murmur of approbation swept over the crowd.

The Overseer ran his eyes around the room and proceeded, "The next unfortunate to be presented is Moses Barnard, who lost three head milk cows in a barn fire shortly after the New Year. The Overseer recommends the loan of two milk cows from the town stock for the year and that his year taxes be abated as he rebuilds, to be reviewed at next year's meeting." The measure was passed without resistance. Also approved was to continue funding Matthew Child 50 cents per week for supporting his mother in victuals, medicine, and clothes. A meticulous record of every expense the previous year had been submitted by Mr. Childs and reviewed by the Overseer.

How Margery wished she could have stayed in the home she and Nathaniel had lived in so happily. But that was not an option for her. She turned her attention back to Fletcher's words.

"I am next directed to *vendue* to the lowest bidder the citizens of the town who are unable to support themselves and find themselves without a sheltering dwelling. As Overseer of the Poor, I am charged with disposing of these paupers by auction at the cheapest terms possible for a period of one year until the next annual meeting." He took a breath and continued, "They are to be comfortably fed and clothed. Any doctor's bills to be paid by the town. You may recoup expenses by putting the pauper's hands to the tasks necessary in your household and for which they have the ability."

Fletcher straightened his shoulders to better carry the responsibility his office entailed and proceeded, "We have three residents to put out to best advantage for the current year. Firstly, we all know Ben Meakin. Please stand Meakin." A ripple of laughter flowed over occupied benches. Pauper auctions were carried out by towns to house the orphaned, abandoned, or incorrigible. Meakin was the town drunk. He was making what had turned into an annual appearance these past few years.

Meakin's wife had taken the couple's children and fled to her prosperous relations in Rhode Island after their home and barn burned. He was only still walking on this earth because his wife, Constance, had pulled his unconscious body out of the flame-engulfed barn. The fire was believed to have been caused by his pipe dropping in the hay when he passed out while taking a break after the last milking of the day. Meakin wasn't welcome at his in-laws' house. His farm with the skeletons of barn and home had been lost to unpaid taxes. He lacked the initiative to rebuild his life, but would put in a solid day's work if supplied with enough alcohol to keep the tremors away.

"While able-bodied, he is bedeviled with love for the drink," Overseer Fletcher said. He turned to look out across the first floor. "Mr. Harrow, did Meakin earn his keep with you this past year and are you prepared to continue to take Meakin into your household at the same rate?"

Old James Harrow and his wife Claire, who had no sons on their homestead, typically took in the sot, who was a talented husbandman. Meakin, despite or because of his constant state of inebriation, was willing to scale a ladder to the highest branches and pick every last apple before they fell to the ground and rotted come fall. Harrow allowed Meakin two quarts of hard cider each morning to take into the fields and orchards as he worked and a measure of rum come nightfall. This was much more generous than the typical single quart given to farm hands daily.

"Yes, I will take Meakin again," the old man responded as he made his way to his feet. "Meakin did complete the tasks set out for him on the farm, with some considerable skill, particularly with orchard business. However, he did bust a ladder in the fall when he knocked the ladder out from under him while he was high in the limbs and then proceeded to land on it."

Guffaws rolled across the meetinghouse and a voice called out, "What did you expect from the sot?" More laughter rang out. "All right, settle down," Overseer Fletcher rumbled. "Mr. Harrow, I rather think that a broken ladder might be expected. You're lucky he hasn't burned your house down, as he did his own. I recommend an additional fee will not be paid for the loss or repair of the ladder." Fletcher paused and looked out over the assembly of men, "Before this business of Benjamin Meakin is concluded, is there any man in the room who would be willing to take on Meakin for less than the current payment of two dollars a week that Mr. Harrow received last year, and would be received this coming year?" Voices murmured indistinctly, but no one spoke up. Fletcher decreed, "Ben Meakin is hereby bid off by James Harrow to keep for the sum of two dollars per week. Harrow will neither be held responsible for any incurred medical expenses nor will he be reimbursed for broken tools."

During the proceedings, Benjamin Meakin stood as silent and still as the granite stones huddling in the walls that meandered throughout the village. His hands gripped his thighs and he stared straight ahead. Margery examined the broken man surreptitiously. *Was he even listening? Can you drink yourself into deafness and block the jeers of your neighbors? Was he thinking of his wife and children, of his next drink, of his shame, of his hatred for those who judged him? Or maybe he wasn't thinking of anything at all.*

"Next," Overseer Fletcher said, in a tone of voice that might have been attempting a semblance of compassion, "I present Widow Turner, wife of Nathaniel Turner, the faithful town blacksmith who tragically perished some months ago of grievous injuries resulting from a fire in his smithy." He went on, "While neither Nathaniel nor Margery Turner were born of Thorneboro, he derived settlement as the taxpayer on the smithy, land, and cottage owned by his absent uncle. He diligently completed his annual service to the town on road repair and other such civic obligations. Margery Turner derives her settlement rights as wife and therefore dependent of Nathaniel Turner, and has the right to fall upon the town."

"Please stand, Widow Turner," Overseer Fletcher called up into the balcony. Margery rose on trembling legs, her cheeks flushed scarlet as she dwelled in the eyes of the townsmen now considering her future. Without being conscious of doing so, she ran her hand down the front of her black skirt and then reached up and clutched her fichu tight around her neck. Overseer Fletcher paused to muster what he hoped appeared to be a solicitous look. "Widow Turner has since become destitute. She has been an inhabitant of the town of Thorneboro these five years since her marriage and has no living kin in her birth town or any other known town where she can remove herself. The union produced no living child. She has been subject to all the Laws and Custom of the town. She has paid her husband's debts through the forfeiture of most of her worldly goods."

Looking round the room Fletcher appealed, "Widow Turner is healthy," he pointed out. "She is a keen homemaker with great ability for labor. She brings her own bedding and clothing. Who will offer a reasonable sum? The floor is open for your offers and I thank you in advance for your willingness to perhaps provide a roof over a head and hopefully benefit yourselves with the labor, such as these unfortunates are able to offer." He paused and added, "I remind all that the town's paupers are to be treated in a Christian-like manner."

The volume of the room rose considerably and included a few poorly covered snorts and chortles at what could only be lewd comments. Although Margery mercifully could not hear the talk on the main floor, she did overhear two men sitting further down in the balcony. One said, "If I had a wife, there was no way I could bring the Widow Turner into the household and expect a wife to be graceful."

The other jested, "You could exchange out the first one." The two enjoyed a shared chuckle. *Boastful words for two as-yet bachelors.* Margery stared straight ahead, not blinking.

All conversations stilled as a voice called out, "I offer to take the Widow Turner for three dollars and fifty cents a week." The bid came from Jacob Kimball, the tanner, who lived on the outskirts of town, far enough away to keep the stench of his trade away from neighbors. "I can use another hand in the tannery for scraping hides and caring for my apprentices."

"And keeping his bed warm," muttered an anonymous voice loud enough to be heard by many, including Margery. Kimball glared around the room. The tanner was overly sensitive to the fact that no woman had yet consented to become his wife, due to his malodorous profession and equally odious personality.

Margery was regretting the small amount of food she had taken at the tavern, as it now threatened to rise up her throat. Paralyzed with terror, she recalled the unwelcome visit Kimball had paid her shortly after Nathaniel's death.

He had roughly offered marriage and she had gently but firmly refused, giving the excuse that Nathaniel was not a year dead and she had no plans to remarry. Kimball had not taken the rejection well, and when he had heard that she had agreed to be put out for vendue, he was furious that she chose to be a pauper over becoming his wife. She knew what was in store if she were to go to his household and thought she might take her life before such a fate.

"We have an offer of three dollars and fifty cents a week from Jacob Kimball." Overseer Fletcher said less than enthusiastically. "This number is a little high considering you plan on putting her to work in the tannery. Do we have another offer?" Kimball remained standing with his chin raised aggressively into the air. More murmurs stirred the end-of-day fetid air.

"One dollar a week." The voice arose from the other side of the floor. The voice belonged to Samuell Wheeler. There were some in the room who could not remember the last time they had heard the sound of his voice. He went on, "I have need of a caretaker for my old mother, whom I support without aid from the town. Widow Turner can also help with the work of the farm and my mother's needlework craft, now that my mother's hands are crippled with rheumatism."

"Another one trying to buy a wife, I wager," commented the nearby balcony pundit.

"But he can afford to wed and any woman in this village would let him have her, virgin to old maid, single or married," his companion opined.

Samuell Wheeler. His mother had made her wedding bed rug. Hannah Wheeler was renowned for her needlepoint bedcovers and sold them as far as Portsmouth, Exeter, and Concord. This had been Nathaniel's extravagant wedding gift to Margery and the one luxury she could not part with when she had been forced to sell her possessions to pay off Nathaniel's debts.

"That is a reasonable offer. Thank you, Mr. Wheeler. Are there any other offers or counter offers?" Overseer Fletcher inquired without making eye contact with the tanner.

Kimball snorted in disgust and threw Wheeler a withering look across the room. "Anyone offering such a small sum must surely have sin on his mind," he sneered. "No one can keep a pauper for such a fee and not become a pauper himself." He slammed back down onto the bench and crossed his arms.

Margery stole a look at Samuell but his eyes were trained on Fletcher as the overseer called once again, "Are there any other offers for support of the Widow Turner?" There was much rustling in the seats, but no one spoke up. "Then the town consents to accept the bid of one dollar a week from Samuell Wheeler for the care of Widow Turner." Margery fell back onto the pew seat, her brimming eyes trained on her shaking blue-veined hands.

"Please stand up, Agnes Bishop," Overseer Fletcher called up to the balcony and waited. The child sat still as a dappled fawn in tall grass. He repeated the command, but still no movement came from the girl. Margery stood up and gently pulled the girl to her feet, setting her crutch under her arm. The girl turned to put her face in Margery's skirts, but Margery carefully faced her forward, whilst taking hold of the girl's hand.

"Next I present Agnes Bishop. Aged 10," Fletcher announced. "Rufus Bishop has lost his wife in the birthing of a child this past winter and he is unable to provide a healthful environment and care for his remaining progeny. He states he is bound for Portsmouth, for the sea. He states that he plans to return with money and perhaps a wife, after a period of one year or more." He paused, then said, "The Bishop family is of the town and Agnes born here. The child is a cripple, but is of sound mind and may perhaps be trained up in some household arts. With firm training, the girl's service may be worth her support. What Christian man will offer a reasonable sum? The floor is open for your offers."

Feet shuffled and men looked at each other around the room, but no one spoke up. The girl tightened her grip on Margery's hand. "Anyone? Please speak up. We do not expect anyone to take the child at their own expense," Fletcher called. Still silence sat. Margery looked up and across the balcony. She caught Samuell looking at the girl, and then he lifted his eyes to Margery as if searching for an answer. Overseer Fletcher shifted awkwardly from foot to foot.

Samuell stood up and all eyes turned to him. His face was unreadable in the dimness of the balcony. "I will take the girl along with Widow Turner for no additional fee, if the Widow Turner is willing to see to her care," he said. "She can assist my mother with the tasks of the household." He looked to Margery and she nodded her head in agreement." Noises of surprise rose from the crowd.

"Thank you, Mr. Wheeler," said Fletcher, "the town appreciates and accepts your offer."

Margery sent a small but sincere smile to Samuell as she and the girl sat down.

Moderator Judson stood to thank Overseer Fletcher for his work on behalf of the town and spoke loudly to be heard over the men now eager to leave the meetinghouse. "This concludes the business of the town meeting for the Year of Our Lord, 1805. I thank you for your participation and if there is no other business, I make a motion that we adjourn to our homes."

Cries of "Aye" echoed off the whitewashed walls. Coats were buttoned over the winter-flat stomachs of the farmers and the protruding stomachs of merchants. Scarves were wound around dirt-rimmed necks, and hats settled on heads.

Ben Meakin rose and excused himself past Margery and Agnes. He turned back, twisting his hat in his hands. "Good luck and God bless you both," he whispered. Margery watched his slumped shoulders as he traversed the balcony and descended the stairs to join the Harrows.

ARRIVAL AT WHEELER FARM
MARCH 1805

Margery and Agnes continued to sit as the meeting-house cleared out. Samuell rose from his seat, wearing an awkward smile, and approached the gated pew. "Mrs. Turner," he said, "I am pleased to make your acquaintance and I hope you will find my home to be comfortable. I won't lie, there is much work to be done on the farm and my mother can be ... difficult." He continued, "But she is much skilled in needle arts and perhaps you might learn such handiwork." He turned his attention to Agnes. "Do not fear, little one, you are safe."

"My father says I must be helpful and quiet and give you no reason to want to send me away." Agnes whispered, looking up at Samuell for the first time. Samuell opened his mouth, but offered no response.

Samuell turned back to Margery. "Pray, Widow Turner," he asked, "where can we retrieve your belongings?"

"I have a chest stored at the mercantile. The Stantons are expecting me to come by to collect it."

"Then let us fetch the wagon and make haste on this night of wicked weather." Samuell turned, expecting them to follow. Stepping out of the meetinghouse, woman and child drew their hooded cloaks over their heads against a flight of icy snow. Samuell lifted his shoulders in a vain attempt to keep melted snow from finding its way between his coat collar and hat to the back of his neck and down his back.

They met at the shed of wagon bays that had sheltered the horses, carriages, and wagons throughout the day. The warmth of the horses had warmed the enclosure, and the animals had gotten by on nosebags of grain and buckets of water. Samuell removed the blankets from a pair of bay draft horses and prepared the animals for the trip, attaching the traces and tightening straps. While he worked on putting the pair of stout mares to wagon, Margery examined the conveyance. A high box seat on springs for driver and companion sat at the front and an open wagon with raised sides in the back.

Though Margery was not an expert on horses, she knew such draft horses as were before her would be neither fast nor well-gaited. The larger of the two turned its head placidly to look at the two human females and gave a low snort. Margery vacillated on whether to climb into the back of the wagon with Agnes and burrow under their cloaks for the cold ride into the unknown. Her choice was made for her when Samuell turned and extended his hand while gesturing towards the seat.

Margery climbed up and settled on the hard bench and then reached down as Samuell lifted up the child and her small cloth bundle of belongings. Margery could feel the girl's ribs as she pulled Agnes up and set her down next to herself. The young widow pulled the worn knee rug over the two of them, and Samuell hopped up to join them, holding the reins comfortably in his chapped hands.

"What are your horses' names," queried Agnes in a tiny voice.

"My mother named them Demeter and Persephone. They are mother and daughter," Samuell chuckled. "They are strong but they have gentle souls."

"The Greek goddess of agriculture and her daughter," Agnes chirped. Margery and Samuell exchanged a glace.

"Quite so, little one. How did you come to learn Greek mythology?" the farmer asked.

"My mother used to tell me stories about the Greek heroes. The story of Demeter and Persephone is very sad." replied the child.

"Well, yes," said Samuell a bit uncomfortably. "But don't worry about these two. They will always be together on my farm." Agnes's face brightened a bit. "Did she read you your Bible, too?" Samuell inquired.

"Of course." Agnes replied simply and pulled her hood lower over her face.

Samuell clucked his tongue and the pair of horses ambled towards the general store and pulled up to the illuminated building. The shopkeeper, Ephraim Stanton, had just himself returned from the meetinghouse. His wife, Martha, had been in charge while he attended to the day's duties. Margery settled Agnes under the rug, and she and Samuell climbed down from the wagon and climbed the porch stairs. Martha stepped out onto the porch before the two could reach for the door handle.

"Mistress Turner, you'll find your trunk ready to go," Martha said. Margery's trunk sat at the far end of the rock-ing-chair-covered porch. The lid was damp, as the shop mistress had not bothered to cover it as it had sat out all day in the inclement weather.

"Mistress Stanton," Margery replied, "I wanted to express my deepest appreciation for the time I have spent here with you the past few weeks."

Before she could finish, Martha interrupted, "Yes, well you can be on your way now. Best of luck." No well wishes dwelt in her eyes.

The shopmistress turned with a new smiling face towards Samuell. "Mr. Wheeler, I am surprised to see you here, taking Mistress Turner into your home. You are a good and Christian gentleman," she simpered. A colder tone emerged as her eyes narrowed. "I hope your charity will not be a hindrance towards you finding a goodly wife soon," she said.

"Please do not worry yourself on my behalf," Samuell replied, without returning a smile.

Ephraim pushed past his wife, who was blocking the door, and greeted the farmer as well. "Samuell, would you care to join me for a drink after this long day?" he enquired. "Mistress Turner and the little one are welcome to come in as well."

Martha glared at her husband, who refused to turn his head to acknowledge his wife's displeasure. "Thank you kindly, but with this weather, we need to be on our way," Samuell responded, hoisting Margery's trunk onto his shoulders. No offer of help came from the diminutive shopkeeper, and Samuell carried the chest down the stairs and placed it in the bed of the wagon.

"Mr. Stanton." Margery said, looking fondly at the shopkeeper, "I sincerely thank you for your hospitality and kindness these past few weeks. I will be forever in your debt."

"Of course, my dear. Best of luck to you," the shopkeeper responded with a sincerity diametric to his wife's hostility.

While a shrewd businessman, Mr. Stanton was henpecked by his wife, whose primary goal in life was to see her two daughters married above their station. She seemed to think the Widow Turner was competition towards her goal, even as Margery had reassured the woman she had no plans to ever remarry. There had been nothing Margery could do to reverse Mrs. Stanton's misplaced antipathy. Mrs. Stanton had counted the days until town meeting when she would be rid of the young widow and had forbidden her husband from bidding at the pauper auction, even though they could use a permanent additional hand in their busy store.

The Stanton girls had not been raised to work behind the counter and would only be called down to the store by their mother if a gentleman deemed eligible came in to make purchases. Mr. Stanton had felt sympathy for the widow and regretted his wife's ill treatment of Margery, ineffectually asking her to show some kindness to a woman who had so unexpectedly lost her husband and her home. He also felt a degree of remorse for having allowed Nathaniel Turner to run up a high tab, and for selling him the many extravagant items Nathaniel couldn't resist buying for his wife.

Margery could not know what the future would bring, but she was quite relieved to be leaving the Stanton's home. Although the scant travelers who passed through town would typically stay at the tavern, she had used her last dwindling coins to rent a room and take meals with the Stantons, who had an extra room in the attic. She also helped out in the store, asking for no discount on her room and board. She had paid in full the debt that Nathaniel had racked up at the store through the sale of Nathaniel's blacksmithing tools and most of her household objects.

"Come now, Ephraim, it's the devil's own weather out here," Martha said, pulling her husband across the threshold into the warmth of their proper family. The shopmistress thudded the door shut against the brutal night and the unwelcome widow.

The sky was quickly darkening, and Samuell lit the two wagon lanterns before climbing back into the driver's seat next to Margery and Agnes. With a clucked command and flick of the reins, he urged the mares down the road that headed out of town and towards the north. The three rode in silence, passing slumbering fields and candle-lit farmhouses where no doubt the men were relating news of the meeting to their wives. Margery's ears burned.

The noxious fumes from the tanning yard assaulted their nostrils far before their eyes set sight on Kimball's place. The smell of rotting flesh and the lime and feces used to soak and soften the leather hides in the tanning yard was abusive. It was the price to pay for leather, a valuable commodity needed by every town resident. Another by-product of the tannery was horsehair, used to stuff plastered walls. Margery felt a pang of pity for the tanner's trade apprentices, who were sent as early as the age of eight to the tanner to help wash, soak, and scrape hair, fat, and tissue from the animal hides. It was some distance before the trio began breathing easily.

Samuell's silence was intimidating, and Margery's mind raced with imagined scenarios of her new situation. The icy pellets bit her face, and the mire of mud and animal waste on the road foully flung itself up the sides of the wagon, reaching for her skirts. Mercifully, they finally came to a collection of buildings looming on the east side of the road, a faint light beckoning from a glass window. As she looked out from her perch, Margery saw a two-story house with a kitchen ell, outbuildings, a solid barn, and doubtless summer-bountiful fields and orchards in the gloaming. Samuell turned right, pulled up into a dooryard, and unnecessarily called out a "whoa" to the animals, who knew they were home.

Raw mud gripped her boots as Margery climbed down off the wagon. Hoof and boot prints around the house and barn were tiny lakes sheeted over with thin ice, ready to crack and drown an unwary shoe. The glow from a window, no doubt a crackling fire in the hearth, promised warmth but not necessarily a warm welcome.

"Can you help the girl while I wipe down the horses?" Samuell asked Margery. He lifted the shivering girl off the seat and placed her non-too-gently on her feet. "Let yourself in," he said. "Try not to startle Mother." He turned away, grabbed Demeter's bridle, and headed for the carriage shed to unhitch the wagon and then on to the barn to curry and bait the horses.

The farmhouse had a formal front entrance with a simple pediment and double doors that faced the road. The house's granite slab stoop was covered with a blanket of slush. No footprints had disturbed this entryway. Margery steadied the child and looked further at the house. The kitchen ell facing the dooryard where she now stood had a simple single door fronted with muddy tracks.

Margery headed in this direction, tugging on Agnes's free hand. Tears welled at the sight of the fine wrought iron thumb latch gracing the door. Nathaniel's work. She hesitated at the door and after a moment's deliberation, knocked on the dark, water-stained wood. She heard a muted voice but no footsteps. She waited a bit and then opened the door, calling in, "Pray pardon, Mistress."

"Yes, yes, I said come in. I can't come to you," she heard. "Bloody screws have made me an old woman. Shut the door. We've had a plentiful harvest of snow this year and the bounty is not yet run out." Margery's grandmother had also suffered from rheumatism, or screws, as the older generation referred to the malady, and she knew the debilitating nature of the disease. Looking towards the source of the voice, Margery saw an old woman sitting in a fanback windsor chair with a writing arm next to the open hearth. Journal, bottle, and quill sat upon the writing surface. How odd to find a writing chair in a kitchen. To have a woman sitting in it was even more astonishing. Margery noticed that the book's open page did not contain writing, but rather a botanical sketch.

As Margery drew closer, she saw keen eyes looking out from a face framed by a white mane and topped with a gathered cap. "Good Evening Mistress," she said. "My name is Margery Turner. Your son has brought myself and this child to your home to be of assistance to you in payment for shelter and food. I am widowed this past year of Nathaniel Turner, the blacksmith." Margery peeled the child's grasping fingers from her own.

The woman in the chair peered at the two closely. "I told my son to find an able-bodied man or woman to help us on this farm. I don't recall asking him to bring me a little one more twisted than I am," the old woman groused.

The old woman looked again at the child with eyes kinder than her words. "What is your name, little tanglefoot?" The child hid her face in Margery's dress. "Look, little tanglefoot, I have knees that look like hubbard squash. Come over and take a look if you don't believe me."

The child peeked out, her curiosity piqued. She leaned down into her hand-carved crutch and swung over, adept in her movement on the solid wood floor, and stopped in front of the old woman. The child opened her mouth but did not gasp as the old woman lifted her layers of apron, skirt, and petticoat, revealing swollen, gnarled knees that indeed resembled the unlovely vegetable.

The old woman dropped the cloth back over her knees and reached alongside her chair and brought out a wooden cane. The burl capping the stick was polished smooth. "My son, the man who brought you to this home, carved this for me so I can get around. Maybe he can make you something a little bigger, as you seem to have grown too tall for your crutch. Now, tell me your name so I don't have to call you 'tanglefoot.'"

"Agnes Bishop," the child murmured.

"That's better." The old woman lifted her eyes back to Margery. "I am Hannah Wheeler. You may call me Mistress Wheeler. Now, help me put out some supper."

Hannah motioned to Agnes to swing the pot hanging from the fireplace crane off the fire, and Margery walked over to lift the heavy pot and carry it to a rough table. The smell of venison stew was comforting. The old woman motioned with her cane to a cupboard with simple but finely-made tableware and Margery ladled the stew into four bowls.

"There is cider in the barrel and the poker is ready in the fire," Hannah instructed.

Margery poured the hard cider from the barrel into a jug and picked up the red-hot iron poker from the embers. Knocking ash off the tip, she thrust the metal rod into the earthenware jug and warmed the liquid. With laborious effort, Hannah rose from the chair by the capacious hearth and came to the table.

The door shuddered open. Samuell and the raw weather entered the room. He was carrying Margery's trunk on one shoulder, and man and chest were too big for the homey, low-ceiled kitchen. "Mother," he greeted, and passed the three into the front of the house. Margery heard the creaking of protesting stairs and a thud of the trunk being deposited onto the floor. The floors complained again with footsteps and Samuell reappeared in the kitchen. The farmer sat down, and pulled a bowl of the pottage towards his place. He took a piece of cornbread from a pan on the table and crumbled it on top of the stew. Margery removed the poker from the cider and poured the warm beverage into cups and placed them on the table. They ate in unfamiliar silence until Samuell abruptly stood up and walked out the door.

"Don't mind Samuell. He's not particularly a talker," Hannah mused. "We won't see him again until morning. It's lambing season, and Samuell worries. He likes to be there to help out any of the mothers having difficult births and making sure the wee little ones are warmly tucked in. Agnes's face brightened, and Margery nodded. "No need to go out to the well. Samuell collected water this morning before he left." She indicated a bucket next to the dry sink.

Without being asked, Margery and Agnes stood up and collected and cleaned the dishes. The child had good intentions, but was of limited use with one hand on her crutch.

"When you are finished here," Hannah instructed, "fill the bed-warming pan and rake and bank the coals. The woodshed and the necessary are out back," she added, pointing to the north side of the buildings. "I sleep in the parlor bedstead and Samuell is in the south bedroom upstairs. There are two small rooms on the north side and the two of you can sleep in the front room." She continued, "In lambing season you can just use the warming pans in my bed and your bed. Samuell will take care of his own, whenever he returns for the night. Close the shutters in the evening and open them in the morning. As the sun rises, I will expect you to stir up the fire." The old woman spoke decisively, but not harshly. "Tonight, put some oat porridge in the coals for the morning."

Margery would have offered to do these household chores and chafed at being ordered. She kept her expression neutral and nodded.

The old woman added, "I know who you are and what happened to your husband. I know you had your own household, and it is going to be difficult to adapt to working for someone else." Hannah went on to repeat Samuell's forewarning, "I won't deny the work is hard and there is plenty of it." She continued, "We had a brother and sister hired out from a farm down the road. But their mother is poorly and they have returned home. But I'm hoping you and I can come to an agreement and work together to help Samuell run this farm. He is the hardest of workers, but there are more chores to do than hours in the day."

"I'm prepared to work to the best of my abilities and I do appreciate your family offering me shelter," Margery assured the old woman and perhaps herself. She added, "I hope to cause you no worriment."

The young widow and child began the evening routines as Mistress Wheeler creakingly prepared to turn in. Farmers, Margery knew, slept and woke by sundown and sunrise. Agnes was tidying the kitchen as well as she could manage. Margery could hear small snuffles and knew the child was shedding tears. She could well imagine the girl's overwhelming feelings as she faced the realization that she was now to live among strangers. Surely tonight would be the first time sleeping away from her family home.

Margery brought the copper warming pan and a chamber stick with a tallow candle to light the way to the parlor. As she closed the shutters inside the parlor, she surreptitiously examined Hannah's tester bed. Columns supported the elaborate textile canopy and hangings that enclosed the bed. A magnificent bed rug, surely Hannah's own work, topped the mattress.

As with families all over New England, the finest bed and bedding were in the parlor, on view for visitors and symbols of the farm's prosperity. Margery mused that the textiles must surely be the most valuable possessions of the Wheeler Farm. Pulling back the drapes enclosing the bedstead, she ran the pan under the layers of sheet, counterpane, and bed rug lying atop the goose feather-filled mattress.

She then brought the pan upstairs. A large bedroom with a hearth was situated in the room above the parlor. On the other side of the hall were two small bedrooms, these with straw-filled mattresses and topped with homespun blankets. In these two compact chambers, strings of dried apple, pumpkin, and bouquets of dried herbs hung from the rafters, as they also did in the kitchen. A handful of somewhat desiccated squashes were stacked in the corner, hiding from the mice and other varmints that inhabited the cellar and barn.

Margery ran the bed warmer through the bed she and Agnes were to use. She returned the pan to the kitchen, adding the coals to the ash-covered nest that would start tomorrow's fire in the hearth. The young widow walked over to the parlor doorway to bid Mistress Wheeler good night as she prepared to retire. Hannah raised her head, looked directly at Margery and asked, "Do you still have the bed rug?" Margery nodded mutely. "Your husband was mighty proud of that wedding present. He pestered me something fierce to have it done in time for your nuptials," Hannah smiled at the memory of the eager young man.

Unwelcome hot tears brimmed and fell down the young widow's cheeks, the drops cooling quickly in the winter-cold house. She could not make a response so she turned from the doorway and collected Agnes to retire upstairs. Margery followed patiently behind the girl stepping and dragging herself up the stairs. The two began to prepare for bed, removing their shortgowns and drawstring skirts, but retaining some layers of shifts and stockings. Margery was relieved to see Agnes had a snug nightcap, retrieved from her modest cloth sack of belongings.

Margery opened the trunk that Samuell had carried in upon returning from putting up the horses. Lying on top was the bed rug that Samuell had commissioned as her wedding present. She had needed to replace the linen sheets of her marital bed after it served as Nathaniel's sick bed. However, the bed rug was unharmed. As the accident had happened in the warmer part of the year, the bed rug had not been lying on the bedstead when he was carried in and placed on the bed, never to rise in this life again. Margery lifted the cover out of the trunk and resisted the urge to smell it. She knew the smell of the fire would overpower any scent of her husband. The smell had seeped into every corner and every textile object in the house.

The familiar stone lay heavy on her heart. Margery spread the rug over the counterpane-covered straw mattress and examined it in the dim candlelight. She knew every stitch of the pattern. What an irony that this treasured textile was now back in the house of its creator. She climbed into the bed next to Agnes, both stiff in their strangeness to each other. Agnes was silent and still for a while before Margery felt her softening beside her, and the sound of even breathing rose from the mound that was the petite child.

Margery did not escape into sleep so easily. *How is it I am here in this stranger's house, when I was a beloved wife not so long ago?* She recalled the crude words of the men she'd overheard at town meeting. What were Samuell's intentions? Did he plan to interfere with her, rather than take a wife as a Christian man should? Margery had sworn to never marry again. She also swore to herself as she lay awake in the ice-cold room that she would be no man's whore, even if it meant forfeiting her life.

As she ruminated and the moon rose, she caught the click of the door latch in the kitchen below. She heard Samuell kick off boots and shuffle around the kitchen, and then heavy treads mounted the stairs. She covered her head with the covers and turned to embrace the sleeping child. She heard Samuell pause at the top of the stairs in front of their door. He did not touch the latch, but turned and entered his room and closed his door. Margery breathed a sigh of relief and continued to hold the child who slept, oblivious to the possibility of immediate or merely imagined danger. Selene's chariot had traveled far in its journey across the night sky before Margery fell into an uneasy sleep.

THE STORY OF
MARGERY & NATHANIEL
PART 1

*As rational creatures should we not seriously put it to ourselves.
Can I promise myself another year? Can I certainly say that my existence
shall be prolonged during the next annual circuit of the sun?*

~ Leavitt's Farmer's Almanac, 1805

"Unnatural," Margery's brother spit. "A woman must marry."

His new wife, Jane, pursed her lips and vigorously nodded. Margery and her younger brother Lyman were the two surviving children of Fredrick and Polly Farnsworth. The family ran a prosperous gristmill in the town of Cantwell. In her brother's eyes, this raised the station of their family above the yeoman farmers in the area. Margery and Lyman had just buried their mother after a long illness. She was laid next to her husband, dead these past seven years. Margery had cared for her mother as Lyman had brought in a wife to their home.

While they were fortunate that they had the coin to buy most of their supplies at the general store, Margery felt the burden of her nursing and household duties. Jane was of no help and took herself to be a woman of leisure. Also in the household were the old couple who were hired help, Enoch and Frances. They had tended to the livestock, housekeeping, and cooking since Margery and Lyman were children. Now in their advancing years, the decrepit couple needed constant oversight.

Now that both parents were gone, Lyman was pressing Margery to marry and move out of the house. He had ambitions beyond being a gristmill owner in a mid-sized town in a sparsely settled state. Margery had no interest in becoming any man's wife, but she was faced with few choices, as she had no money or land of her own. It was not considered natural to live alone. Men who were not first-born could undertake an apprenticeship, go to war or to sea, become a minister, or head into the woods to the lumber camps. Unmarried women who left the family home found their choices were much more limited. They could become governesses or teachers if they were schooled, or household or shop help if they were not. Some sold their bodies as commodities, seldom by choice.

"I am taking a teaching position at the new school in Warrington," Margery said. She fisted her hands into her hips as she informed her brother of her plans. By tradition, she should have asked permission.

"You will get none of your dowry money," Lyman threatened. Margery did not reply and returned Lyman's baleful stare. A week later, Margery rode away with her mother's chest holding her few belongings, including her sketch books, charcoal, graphite, and watercolors, and began her life as a schoolmarm.

In Warrington, she rotated among town families for lodging, "boarding round" as was the custom for school masters and mistresses. Boarding in the townspeople's homes, being constantly surrounded by others and expected to make conversation, presented an uncomfortable challenge for the reserved young woman. Margery had been accustomed to her own company when she lived under her parents' roof. She had always had a solitary nature and vastly preferred walking and sketching in the woods or along the river that ran by her parents' gristmill and house to chattering with other girls her age about fashion and boys. Her childhood classmates had been content enough to leave her to her reclusive pursuits.

Before the end of her first year, Margery received a letter from Lyman informing her that he had sold the farm and mill, dismissed the old servants, and that he and Jane were moving to New York. They were to live out their pretensions, and Jane would have soft, white bakery bread every day without having to flour her hands. The brief missive stated that they would write again with their new address in the city, but no further letter ever arrived.

Margery loved teaching but was quite often discouraged. She inevitably faced intractable resistance from the parents of the few gifted students who she recommended to be allowed to continue their studies. Smart or dull, most of her students were expected to live out their lives on their family farms, using their basic literary and arithmetic skills to keep account books tracking the farm's spending and selling, and day books and farm journals documenting farm life and weather. Not all students even made it through the eight grades nestled into the one-room schoolhouse. The school was closed for long periods during planting and harvesting season.

The young schoolmistress looked for and encouraged special aptitudes and interests. She tried her best to foster a love of inquiry and learning. The subjects that parents expected the teacher to cover were reading, writing, arithmetic, and a smattering of history and geography, all infused with moral lessons. Margery added art. She would take the children out into the schoolyard and have them sketch their natural world. In cold weather, she would bring in objects to draw as still lifes. She might place a whole apple and an apple cut in half in front of each student. Allowing the students to eat the pippins after the lesson made them laugh, as it was typically the students who were expected to bring apples to the teacher.

Margery met Nathaniel when she was boarding at the home of Abraham and Clara Wright. Abraham ran the iron foundry in town. Nathaniel traveled frequently to Warrington to buy the metal he used to create his wrought iron latches, hinges, axe heads, cookware, nails, hooks, and other implements. When Nathaniel came to town, he stayed at the tavern. After years of doing business with Abraham, he was in the custom of accepting a dinner invitation to the foundry owner's home after the conclusion of their business dealings.

Clara had mentioned to Margery that there would be an additional guest from Thorneboro joining them for dinner, but the teacher had forgotten over the course of a trying day. A seventh-grade student had climbed the apple tree in the schoolyard, which was strictly prohibited. He had fallen and cracked his collarbone. The boy's sobs, which had quickly ratcheted into shrieks as bravado evaporated and pain intensified, still rung in the teacher's ears.

Margery was reminded of the visitor when Clara prompted her to set an extra place at the table. She noticed that Clara was preparing Marlborough pie, an apple custard pie usually reserved for holidays and guests. Margery heard a knock, followed by the raised and enthusiastic voices of Abraham and his guest.

Abraham called the women out and made the introductions. "Nathaniel Turner," he announced, "may I present Miss Margery Farnsworth, the pretty schoolmarm I told you about." Margery and Nathaniel both blushed deeply, but as she looked at Nathaniel and offered a polite smile, she noticed that a wide grin was sitting in his open face. His eyes were ash grey with flecks of black, and his dark hair was pulled back in a queue.

Over the meal of beef steak pie, potatoes cooked in bacon fat, salet, cheese, squash pudding, stewed pears, and the much-admired Marlborough pie, Margery felt a flush of warmth envelope her entire body, despite being seated furthest away from the dining room fire. Nathaniel was exceedingly polite and proper, but Margery, who tried to keep her eyes on her plate, would glance up and see him smiling towards her. She wondered if he continued to smile at her the whole time, even when she dropped her eyes. But his crooked smile beckoned and warmed her.

Margery, who even in everyday situations needed to push herself to be a charming conversationalist, was tongue-tied.

The men discussed their business and complimented the women on the dinner. Six-year-old Darby nodded off and his head dropped into his half-full plate, providing a shared laugh for the adults. The evening ended pleasantly enough, but as she helped wash dishes, she tuned out Clara's chatter and became preoccupied with the thought that she had acted like one of her schoolgirls at dinner. Her face burned and she felt the fool.

The next morning, Abraham came into the kitchen as the family was breaking fast and informed Margery that the wagon horse's shoe was a bit wobbly, and he would need to take a look at it. He apologized that he would not be able to drive Margery and Darby to school and promised that he would run Darby to school when the shoe was repaired. While staying at the Wrights, Margery had enjoyed the luxury of being driven to school along with first-grader Darby, especially of a cold morning. She nodded and wished Abraham luck with the shoe and departed for the one-mile walk to the schoolhouse.

As she stepped out the door, she was startled to encounter Nathaniel who was rather self-consciously leaning against his iron-filled horse-drawn wagon. "Good morrow, Miss Farnsworth," he grinned. "I am finished with my business here with Mr. Wright and will be returning to Thorneboro today." He hesitated, then asked, "Would you accept my offer of a ride to school?"

Margery turned back towards the house and was quick enough to see Clara and Abraham smiling sheepishly before they dropped the curtain. Margery felt her mouth go dry. "Thank you, good sir," she managed. Margery knew that Nathaniel's route out of town led in the opposite direction from her path. She allowed Nathaniel to hand her up into the box seat. Nathaniel climbed up and sat beside her. The schoolteacher was uncomfortably aware of their thighs in contact within the snug seat. She was surprised to feel no sense of trepidation, as she might have if it had been any other unfamiliar man.

They rode along, Margery holding her cloth-wrapped hot baked potato in her woolen mitts. She would transfer the half-cooked potato to the coals of the school stove, which sat in the center of the room, to have it finished cooking and hot for midday lunch. Nathaniel wore no gloves, and Margery noticed that his roughened hands were laced with burn scars. After a few awkward attempts at conversation petered out, Nathaniel finally succeeded in encouraging Margery to tell him of her students.

As a schoolteacher, she had no shortage of amusing anecdotes about her students. She told of a student who had smuggled in newborn chicks in her lunchpail. Then there was the boy who had fallen asleep, knocked over his inkpot, and stained the entire side of his face. Quill ink, made of ground walnut shell, ash, vinegar, and salt, was quite permanent, and the dye remained on the boy's face for well over a week.

By the time they reached the schoolhouse, Margery realized with embarrassment that she had been doing most of the talking, spurred by Nathaniel's earnest and curious questioning. "You must think me quite the pratepie," Margery blurted. "I did not allow you a word."

"It is as I wished. I wanted to know more of you," Nathaniel soothed as he climbed down from the wagon and came around to offer her a hand to descend. "You can make it up to me."

Margery stiffened. "Sir," she began, drawing back from the extended hand.

"Nathaniel smiled and quickly added, "by allowing me to write to you and perhaps speak to you again on my next buying trip." Margery held her breath a moment before responding, "Yes, I would enjoy that." Her heart was threatening to burst through her chest. She took the proffered hand and climbed down from the wagon, smoothing her skirts as she stood awkwardly before the young man.

Nathaniel bowed in a comical manner, smiled, and vaulted back into the wagon seat. He turned the heads of the pair of dapple-grey horses back towards the road and he called out, "Until we meet again." The young blacksmith rode away, clucking and speaking to his horses, letting them know they were heading home. Margery watched him for a few moments before she went into the schoolhouse to prepare for her new day.

As promised, Nathaniel did indeed write to Margery. His letters told her of days spent at his blacksmith's forge and nights sitting under the stars by the creek that ran behind his smithy and cottage. The letters often included whimsically phonetical spellings of words that Margery had to interpret as best she could. Despite his obvious lack of grammar, his humor and goodness emanated from every page.

Margery found herself falling in love. On his first visit back to town a few months later, they walked out and talked for hours. She told him of her brother selling the farm and moving away, leaving her not a penny. He told her of his life coming to America as a boy to be indentured to his uncle, a blacksmith. His uncle, a royalist, had emigrated to Canada, still under British control, when America won its independence. Nathaniel, having finished his seven-year apprenticeship and now a well-trained blacksmith, had remained and rented from his uncle the blacksmith shop and small adjacent cottage in the town of Thorneboro.

The two were opposite in so many ways. Whereas Nathaniel was full of joy and hope, Margery was more reserved, more suspicious, perhaps even pessimistic. He worked hard to make her laugh, to point out the beauty that was present all around them. The young blacksmith would stop to carry a turtle to the other side of the road to ensure it wouldn't be crushed by a wagon wheel. Nathaniel considered a bouquet of scarlet winterberries an appropriate courting gift. He brought the young schoolmistress whimsical and impractical hand-made gifts, such as a wrought iron heart of scrolled metal. He opened her heart, and she learned to smile and look at the world as a place of wonders, rather than one of cruelty and selfishness, as she had experienced with her brother.

When Nathaniel learned of her avocation for art, he begged for a portrait of her. Just reading the words in the letter with his request made Margery flush with heat and embarrassment. She begged leave to not have to fulfill the request. He was relentless, however, until Margery finally sat down with Clara's borrowed hand mirror to attempt a self-portrait in pencil. Margery did not think she had a hand for drawing the human figure. She preferred sketching botanical still lifes and painting *en plein air*. A cluster of red trillium, known by the unlovely name "stinking Benjamin" or an ephemeral woodland lily would not judge its image as seen through Margery's eyes.

The black and white self-portrait would be a shadow. It would not indicate the color of her solemn hazel eyes, the shade of her primly smooth honey-brown hair, or the frequent blush that swept her cheekbones in awkward social situations. As she looked at herself in the mirror, she could see the struggle raging in her heart. She reeled between feelings of euphoria — "I am loved" and dismal certitude — "Surely such a man cannot truly love me." She had not known that love could be so terrifying and wondered if that feeling would ever go away.

Much precious paper was wasted on drafts violently crumpled and discarded before she had a version she could — if not like — at least accept. She mailed it to Nathaniel the next day, and his return letter waxed ecstatic. As if bathed in warm water by gentle hands, Margery's heart was soothed and she let happiness into her heart.

Nathaniel surprised Margery with a visit in mid-October. He had been in Warrington on a buying trip just two weeks prior, and she knew he could not need additional supplies so soon. On his last visit, Abraham and Clara had made a surprising announcement over dinner.

"We have some news we would like to share with you," Abraham declared over a dessert of bread pudding fragrant with brandy. Margery looked towards Clara, expecting to see a beaming face about to announce another addition coming to the family. But while Clara's face wore a smile, Margery could see that the young woman's eyes were tinged with sorrow.

"What is it!" Nathaniel asked in his now familiar eagerness.

Abraham took a breath and began, "We are selling the house and foundry and moving up to Penobscot Bay. My brother has a thriving shipyard and looks to expand with my help."

Margery knew that the region of Penobscot Bay was in the District of Maine, part of the Commonwealth of Massachusetts, but she knew nothing of the distant towns perched along the Atlantic Sea. She turned to look at Nathaniel. The young man looked confused for a moment, then a sadness entered into his eyes.

"Surely, the new foundry owner will take a liking to you and you will continue to enjoy fair prices and the occasional fine meal," Abraham attempted to jest. Clara's eyes brimmed with tears.

"I am nothing but pleased for your good fortune," Nathaniel forced a grin.

"Margery," Clara interjected. We won't be leaving for a few fortnights. There is much to do to prepare to leave. When you are ready, the Mason family is prepared to put you up."

The Mason family had four children occasionally at the schoolhouse and a pack of younger ones still at their modest farmhouse outside of the town proper. While Margery was grateful to know she would have a roof over her head, she knew the experience of boarding at the Mason's would be one that required of her a significant amount of farmwork, unlike what she experienced in the Wrights' comfortable town house.

The conversation about the impending move continued far into the night. False cheer joined the foursome and only departed when each took to their beds.

Now, two weeks after the Wright's announcement, Nathaniel showed up at the schoolhouse as the young schoolteacher rung the bell to dismiss the children. The boys and girls giggled as they exited and saw their teacher's sweetheart was waiting. After admonishing the students to hurry home to their chores, Margery walked over to Nathaniel, puzzled but pleased.

Nathaniel smiled at her with an uncommon look of nervousness on his face and took both of her hands in his own. Neither had yet spoken a word. Dropping to a bended knee, under the schoolyard apple tree heavy with fruit, Nathaniel asked simply, "Margery will you marry me?" Margery accepted with a mute nod, tears streaming down her face. He stood and took her into his arms, kissing her for the first time and promising a lifetime of more kisses, laughter, and family.

As Margery's parents were dead and her brother disappeared, there was no one for Nathaniel to ask for her hand. He knew she had no dowry, but told her he did not hold with the antiquated and barbaric custom.

Abraham and Clara, who took great pride in their role introducing the couple, insisted the wedding and reception be held in their home on the night of Thanksgiving. Margery wore her best blue woolen gown, and Nathaniel wore his only wool broadcloth suit. Nathaniel had crafted a wedding ring for Margery in his blacksmith shop from a gold coin. An inscription inside the gold band read *Forever My Heart and Home.* The wedding dinner included roast pig, roast turkey, onions in cream sauce, parsnips in butter, Indian pudding, cranberry sauce and cranberry tart, pumpion pie, apples, and nuts. The holiday food was accompanied by spiced rum punch in Clara's prized Canton rose famille punchbowl and tankards of hard cider.

Glasses and tankards were raised over and over again to cheer the couple's union.

Clara had also baked a dense bride's cake brimming with raisins, currants, almonds, and citron. In it hid a whole nutmeg. By tradition, the person who received the slice with the fragrant seed was destined to be the next married. As the guests enjoyed the cake, no one was fessing up to finding the nutmeg. Clara finally cried, "Out with it. Who has the nutmeg?"

Abraham looked around the room and spied the desperate face and flaming red cheeks of his young son. "Darby, my lad. Is it you?" he called. The father ran over to pry open the boy's clenched fist holding the spice.

"I don't want to get married," Darby wailed, and ran crying from the room. The adults roared with laughter.

"Aye, someday he will be quite keen on it," Nathaniel joked and beamed at his new wife.

Margery's students came to the house to present her with a hand-bound book they had crafted containing prayers, moral lessons, sketches, and wishes for happiness. The children were given sweetmeats from Clara. Many of the students, even some of the typically stoic boys, had tears in their eyes as they bid their teacher farewell and congratulations.

The wedding party lasted until late in the evening. "You must take our bed tonight," Abraham insisted. "It has brought us great joy and our precious Darby," he chuckled, as he wrapped his bear-like arm around his wife. They would accept no objection from Nathaniel. Conscious of the house full of people, Margery and Nathaniel retired and chastely fell asleep with hands clasped and hope held tight.

In the morning, they packed Nathaniel's cart and departed for Thorneboro to cries of well-wishes. Margery presented Abraham and Clara with a sketch of Darby sitting proudly on his pony. She had sworn the boy to secrecy when she asked him to pose, and somehow, he had kept quiet. It was more likely the child had forgotten about the afternoon he was asked to sit on his pony for a boring half hour. The newlyweds drove with legs and hips bumping under the rug through a morning capped with a bluebird sky. The early snow glittered as if scattered with diamonds.

Nathaniel talked, sang, and talked some more. His heart was an open book. He shared his dreams for their future and prompted Margery to tell him how he could make his house into their home. Margery was faint with the powerful feelings welling in her breast. She knew she was happy. She knew she was blessed. She was excited for the future, and she felt content and safe in Nathaniel's devotion. She wanted to be the best wife she could be to this good, good man. The new wife tried to tamp down the unwelcome and occasional flicker of fear, a wave of gooseflesh rolling over her arm. *Can my good fortune truly be trusted?*

As they approached the village of Thorneboro, Nathaniel began recognizing a few fellow travelers on the road. He greeted the men heartily by name, and sober hands were raised in return. The newlyweds passed the saw mill along the river and entered the town. They rode by the meetinghouse, tavern, and general store. Margery noted a wheelwright shop, a furniture maker, shoemaker, and butcher. Then the blacksmith's foundry and cottage came into view.

The smithy looked as if it had been smoked like a ham. Dark walls and large doors would open into a courtyard when the smith was at work. Once an apprentice himself, Nathaniel had now taken as his apprentice a young boy from town. "Aaron is a hard worker," the blacksmith assured his new wife, "surely not sleeping up in the garret under sloping eaves of the roof this late in the morning, but certainly out gathering wood."

He brought the wagon and horses around to the back of the building where there was a small stable, carriage shed, and a private entrance to the modest living quarters across the yard from the smithy. "Stay seated," Nathaniel pleaded with a hand up. He jumped from the wagon, pulling an iron key from a pocket. He unlocked the door, kicked it open, and ran back to Margery. He opened his arms and said invitingly, "Mistress Turner, let me carry you into your new home."

With a giggle, Margery lowered herself into Nathaniel's arms. He kissed the top of her head, swung her around and bounded into the house, knocking Margery's ankle rather sharply against the doorjamb. She swallowed a cry of pain and laughed as he placed her on her feet in the low-roofed kitchen. He declared, "I send my uncle payments for the use of the house and the shop and I pay the town all taxes due on the property. One day it will be ours – free and clear." He lowered his head for a tender kiss but soon pulled away and cried, "A tour for the lady of the house."

"I made these kitchen tools for you," Nathaniel pointed proudly at a kettle hanging from the iron crane arm and trammel hook in the brick fireplace. A dutch oven and spider skillet sat on the stone floor of the fireplace. Also present were ladles, skimmer, skewers, flatware, a gridiron and even a toasting iron.

"They are very fine work," Margery enthused.

There was also a gleaming copper kettle, new redware mugs, and pewter plates and platters, certainly from the village store.

"My uncle took the furnishings with him," Nathaniel explained. "I made tools for the cabinetmaker in exchange for the kitchen table and chairs and a bedchamber table and chair. There is soon to be a chest of drawers for the bedchamber as well."

Margery noticed that there was no sign of the touch of a cook. No herbs hung from the ceiling, no dried apples strung up on a string, no crocks of pickled produce, no barrel of cornmeal. As if reading her mind, Nathaniel said, "I'm sure there are plenty more things you need here in the kitchen. I have been taking my meals at the tavern since my uncle moved."

"Isn't that rather expensive," Margery inquired.

"Well, yes, I guess it is." Nathaniel said with a good-humored shrug.

Nathaniel pulled Margery along into the bedroom. Brass candlesticks and a warming pan glinted. The bed-rope tightener sat on a candle stand. A porcelain chamber pot peeked out from under the bed. A rope-strung bedstead held a fresh tick mattress filled with feathers and covered with an intricately-woven bed rug of needle-worked wool topped the bed.

"Oh Nathaniel. This is magnificent," Margery said, approaching the bed and reverently stroking the textile. The design featured a potted apple tree heavy with fruit. Winding branches of apple blossoms made up the border, and the date 1801 was woven into the head of the spread. The foundation was black, making the botanical motif appear to lift off the background.

"There is a woman in this very town, Hannah Wheeler, who makes these rugs," he explained. "You must have something very fine to lie under. I made door hinges and latches for her house in exchange."

"My darling, it is I who was required to furnish our home with my marriage portion," Margery fretted.

Nathaniel quieted her with a kiss. "Margery, give no more thought on that and don't let it pain you," he said. "You know I do not hold with such traditions. You are my most precious gift and I will strive to give you everything to make your life one of comfort."

"My darling, I don't have a need for such splendid things. I just have a need for you."

They reached for each other with beating hearts and trembling hands and lay together for the first time as man and wife.

THE STORY OF
MARGERY & NATHANIEL
PART 2

"I think Aaron might have a sweetheart." Margery confided her suspicion to Nathaniel over breakfast.

"Indeed, pray share with me the signs that you have observed," Nathaniel chuckled.

"He smiles at secret thoughts and moves as if he is in a dream. He comes down in the morning looking as if he has not slept a wink. Have you not noticed this about the boy?" Margery queried.

"Aye, I should recognize the symptoms, having been infected with a severe case of love sickness that still to this day afflicts me," Nathaniel said, throwing his forearm to his head to mimic a swoon.

"He has recently started asking me if I need anything fetched from the butcher," Margery insisted.

"Ah, my dear, that is verily suspicious. Although he is a decent worker, he is not one to volunteer for additional chores," Nathaniel noted and winked.

"When I did assent to sending him for some salt pork the other day, he washed his face before he left."

"The boy must have a sweetheart! Perchance it may be Molly, the butcher's girl?"

"That would be my guess," Margery concurred.

"Ah, young love," Nathaniel sighed and stood from the table to head to the blacksmith shop, where Aaron would have the coals stoked and ready for the day's work. He kissed Margery, grabbed his account book, ducked through the doorway, and walked across the dooryard to the smithy. Soon after, Margery heard the sound of hammer on anvil as the day's work began. She knew Nathaniel had a harrow to repair and two axe heads to make for Caleb Williams. Matthew Child had ordered 200 nails, which Aaron could make.

Come midday dinner, she heard Nathaniel whistling as he crossed back toward the house. As he removed and hung up his leather apron and washed up, she hurried to the forge to deliver Aaron a covered plate, as the fire in the forge could not be left unattended. Margery and Nathaniel also enjoyed the privacy of having the house to themselves each midday, and today, as on many days, they followed their meal with a sweet interlude of lovemaking. They were straightening their clothes when Margery smelled a strong scent of wood fire, which was a sweeter scent than the coal fire in the smithy hearth. The smell of wood fire was, of course, ubiquitous in a village where every home cooked and heated with wood, but this was far more overpowering and near.

She peered out the window and panic gripped her throat as she saw flames leaping out of the smithy. She screamed, "Nathaniel!" The blacksmith had seen the sight over her shoulder and was already sprinting out of the room. She followed him, and as she reached the doorway, she saw Nathaniel racing towards the burning building calling, "Aaron, Aaron!" There was no sign of the young man. The crackling and cackling flames sheeted the sky. Nathaniel peered into the inferno, trying to spy the boy. Margery saw what he was planning on doing and shrieked, "Nathaniel, NO!" She watched in terror as he hunched his shoulders and plunged into the burning building.

By this time, neighbors were running in with buckets to form a brigade to bring up water from the creek behind the cottage. Margery ran towards the flame-engulfed structure, but fell back as a central beam came down, pushing out fire and sparks through the wide-open doors. She thought she was screaming, but heard no sound from her open mouth. As she scrambled to her feet, she saw Nathaniel exit the building carrying the limp and blackened form of Aaron.

Nathaniel was on fire. His clothes and his hair were alight. He dropped Aaron and fell to his knees. Margery ran to him, tearing off her apron. She covered her husband's body, beating to snuff out the flames. Nathaniel rolled onto the ground without an utterance, with eyes staring at the sky. His chest heaved. Nathaniel was alive. Margery looked over at Aaron and saw open, unblinking eyes and knew the boy was dead.

Margery called to two men just running in from the street, "Help me carry Master Turner to his bed." The men struggled under the weight of his motionless, solid body as they transported the blacksmith into the house. Margery grabbed the sleeve of her neighbor Mistress Freeman, who was standing in the middle of the dooryard and staring agape at the inferno. She begged the stunned woman to run for the doctor. Margery followed the men into the house and instructed them to lay Nathaniel on the cool linen sheets.

Nathaniel's eyes were open and his breath was ragged, but he did not respond to her as she called his name. The men departed. Margery ran to the kitchen and returned with cloths and a bucket of cool water from a barrel in the kitchen. She retrieved her sewing scissors from her sewing kit and cut away what was left of his clothes. His leather apron would have protected his chest, but he had left it behind in his haste to rescue Aaron.

Nathaniel's hair was gone and his head was covered in blotchy, raw patches. On his lower arms and hands, his skin had completely burned off, and Margery could see the white of his wrist bone on one hand. On his face, his eyebrows and eyelashes were gone, and blistering had already begun. His chest was white and black where once lay rosy skin and bristly hair. Margery felt completely overwhelmed. She began trying to wash him, but hesitated where the skin was gone. A musky, charcoal smell enveloped the room, and it took Margery significant effort not to gag. Nathaniel's breathing was becoming more labored, and with every hitch of breath, Margery's fear notched a bit higher.

Outside the window, Margery heard the sound of keening and recognized the voice of Molly, the butcher's girl and Aaron's suspected sweetheart. It was the sound of a heart shattered. Margery felt her heart miss a beat in sympathetic pain, but she closed her ears, as there was nothing she could do now for Aaron. Was there anything she could do for her own husband clinging to life?

Doctor Caswell came into the room then, and Margery felt a wave of gratitude and hope break over her. He examined the still, silent Nathaniel and then turned a grim face towards Margery. "I can give him laudanum to ease some of the pain," the doctor stated, "but I won't be able to remove the pain completely. You can continue to wash as you are able, and then he needs to have his burns covered in lime-water liniment mixed with linseed oil and then wrapped in clean linen. I will send my girl over with what you need as soon as I return to my farm. I can't tell you if he will live or die."

We, not he. We. Margery corrected the doctor in her mind. She knelt next to the bed, and swallowing the quaver that threatened her voice, said, "Nathaniel, you will recover. All is well. I love you. I am here." The physician left Margery alone with her grievously injured husband.

Dr. Sampson Caswell had begun his career in medicine during his time in the Continental Army. Before his return from war, the midwife Sarah Bradford cared for the sick and injured of the town and attended both births and deaths. When Caswell moved to Thorneboro, the relationship between the two healers was surprisingly cooperative. Sarah was heading towards the time of her own aged infirmary. With generosity, she taught the new, informally-trained doctor and shared her hard-earned medical lore. She continued to attend births while Caswell took over other patient needs until she passed away. He was a competent physician, but not a miracle worker.

The next days were Sisyphean cycles of changing dressings, dribbling broth into her husband's mouth, administering laudanum, and trying to get Nathaniel to speak. Some of the townswomen came by with fresh linens, food, and advice. The blacksmith shop fire had been put out, but smoke still rose from its charred skeleton.

On the third day, Nathaniel turned his head as Margery knelt by his bedside and repeated her mantra, 'Nathaniel, you will recover. All is well. I love you. I am here."

His red eyes gazed out from a ravaged face and he whispered, "I'm sorry." A tear rolled down his cheek and he turned his face to the wall.

"Oh, my darling. No, No. No. There is nothing to be sorry for. You soon will be well and we will be well."

On the fifth day Nathaniel could not open his mouth to receive broth. His jaw clenched, and a thread of drool slipped down his chin. His neck muscles appeared to be tightening. Margery sent for the doctor, who examined Nathaniel once again and turned to Margery without making eye contact. "Nathaniel has lockjaw," he told her, "which makes me believe he has tetanus. You must prepare yourself, as few can recover from this affliction. He may start to writhe and may lose control of his breathing or even his night soil and water."

Margery's eyes widened in horror. "You must cure him," she pleaded.

"I'm afraid I cannot. We can give him more laudanum to relieve some pain, but there is no cure."

The next few days were a hell far surpassing any of Homer's description of the underworld. Nathaniel's face settled into a grimace, his fists remained clenched, and his body rocked. He arched off the bed as if racked, and the spasms would have snapped the bones and spine of a weaker man. Margery began to pray for her beloved husband's release from his torment and wished the two of them could depart to eternal peace together.

This good, gentle man,
who would stop mid-stride to listen to a songbird.
This good, loving man,
who loved Margery unreservedly.
This good, generous man,
who cared not that Margery had no bridal portion.
This good, jolly man,
who made Margery laugh.
This good, trusting man,
who believed in the honesty of his neighbors.
This good, heroic man,
who ran into a burning building to save a careless lad.
This good, good man,
who was tortured as if thrown into the deepest depths
of Tartarus.

Something in Margery was breaking as well, perhaps never to heal. On the eighth day, Nathaniel died in agony, with Margery beside him.

Nathaniel was laid to rest in the burial ground alongside the Thorneboro Meetinghouse, nestled among young and old who had gone to their maker in various states of grace. Margery donned a simple black mourning dress and tied the window shutters closed with black ribbon. She ordered a slate headstone, firmly refusing the winged skulls or cherubs favored by the older town residents, or the newly-popular urn and willow decorations gracing the stones of those recently departed. An anvil, tongs, and hammer would grace her husband's stone with the simple carved epitaph.

Nathaniel Turner

Beloved Husband of Margery

The roaring fire of your forge has gone cold.
Your hammer has ceased its mighty thunder.
Yet your memory lives on in my heart
until we meet again.

Departed this life on the 27th day of July, 1804

Aged 28 years

For the week after the funeral, more often than not, Margery sat as if paralyzed in the kitchen next to a cold hearth. She rose only to answer the door to accept un-wanted gifts of food and quietly mumbled condolences from the neighbors. At night, she slept wrapped in the bed rug, having had to burn the blood-and -pus-soaked bedding used during Nathaniel's confinement. On the Sunday following Nathaniel's funeral, Margery heard the meeting-house bell ring, calling worshipers. She sat up with a mind not to attend service but rather write to Nathaniel's uncle in Canada to tell him of his nephew's death.

On the following day, Margery went to Stanton's General Store to mail the letter. Mistress Stanton was minding the counter when Margery came in. She handed the storekeeper her letter.

"My sympathies, Widow Turner. Master Turner was a good man," said Mistress Stanton, taking the sealed missive. "This letter will go out by post tomorrow. Do you need anything else today?"

"Thank you. I am not in need of anything else today," the new widow replied.

As she turned to the door, she heard Mistress Stanton clear her throat and continue, "Now that you are in charge of your own housekeeping, I thought you might want a copy of your account, as it stands." She handed Margery a folded piece of paper. Margery opened and read the sheet, drew in a sharp breath, bid the shopkeeper a good day, and walked out the door.

Seated at her kitchen table, door bolted shut, Margery once again opened the accounting tally from the store. Could the sums on the page be accurate? While Margery visited the store for food and household items, Nathaniel was the one who brought in his iron work for barter or cash when paid in coin by his customers, to put towards their tab. Margery was speechless at the lengthy list of charges carried on credit and the amount of debt they had acquired. She thought of Nathaniel's extravagant wedding gifts and frequent presents from Stanton's that he brought home to her without a thought to cost. Were there other outstanding debts to the tradesmen in town? She was expecting charges for the physic, headstone, coffin, winding sheet, in addition to the rum and other libations consumed at the tavern following Nathaniel's funeral.

Nathaniel's account book for the blacksmith business, documenting who had paid with cash or owed on credit, had burned in the fire. No townsperson had come to her door seeking to settle up their debt, and Margery wondered how many would "forget" they had owed Nathaniel money for jobs done.

Margery began to bring household items to Stanton's — her brass candlesticks, fine iron cutlery, tableware, and other housewares to pay off her debt. Little could be salvaged from the smithy. A cold terror settled over her as she read the letter she received back from Nathaniel's uncle, who owned the house. He wrote of his true sorrow over the death of his nephew.

Perhaps thinking himself quite generous, he offered that Margery could live in the house for another few months before she moved back to her family. He would then sell the house. Nathaniel's uncle had no idea she didn't have a family to whom she could return. She pondered if she should write to him to make him aware of this fact, but she had never even met this man or his wife, and surely they would not consider offering her a place in their home in Canada.

If Nathaniel had owned the house and blacksmith forge outright, rather than paying his uncle rent, Margery would have been granted a widow's right of dower. This law held that a widow had a right to one third of the property owned by her husband with tenancy granted for the length of her lifetime. Even in the case of insolvency, the widow received her portion before creditors were paid. Widows who did not remarry often took in lodgers as a source of income. There was no right of dower available to Margery.

A few townsmen eventually came to her door with payments owned to Nathaniel, but she knew not all had come. She never let anyone enter the house, but stood in her doorway to accept condolences. The young widow would bring items into the dooryard to exchange for coin when someone asked her about purchasing Nathaniel's clothes or tools that had survived the fire. It broke her heart to part with her husband's belongings, but what could she do?

Margery was in her kitchen on a late summer day of sheeting rain and battering winds when a knock on the door startled her. As she opened the door, she could identify the visitor by smell, rather than by the face, which was hidden under a hooded cloak.

"Ah, Widow Turner," the caller said. "I come to offer my sympathies and make good on my debt owed to your late husband."

Margery stood in the doorway as the rain sluiced off the man's cloak. Thunder rumbled close at hand, and she wondered what would make the man come out in such wicked weather. She was distressed to realize she would have to invite the man in.

"Master Kimball, won't you come in," she said, motioning unenthusiastically for the tanner to enter.

He and his stench stepped through the doorway. He removed his sodden cape and hung it on a hook by the hearth. "Thank you kindly, good lady. It is hunch-weather, to be sure."

Jacob Kimball smiled expectantly in her direction, forcing her by custom to offer, "Shall I warm some cider?"

"That would do very well indeed. I thank you for your hospitality," the tanner replied.

He seated himself at the table, pushed the widow's work aside, and ran his eyes over her form. She sighed inside and recalled that the tanner never looked when he could leer. All the women and girls in the town knew this to be true.

"As you know," he began, as Margery warmed a cup of cider drawn from a jug, "Nathaniel was my great friend." Margery worked hard to keep her face from registering her reaction, which was one of anger at this empty and untrue statement. "I can remember our time spent in the tavern before he married you. We often sat near each other in the bachelor's balcony of the meetinghouse," he waxed. The tanner was yet unmarried, unable to find a wife who would live in the fetid atmosphere of a tanner's yard.

Margery put the mug in front of the man and remained standing. Kimball continued, "I bring coin for the knives and hooks Nathaniel forged for me last winter. I was to trade him for leather to make a new smithy apron and britches, but he no longer needs those earthly goods, now does he?" He furrowed his brows and stuck out his lower lip in a pantomime of grief. Margery's stomach turned.

He went on, "I hear that you will need to be leaving Nathaniel's uncle's house. It is indeed a pitiable situation." He appraised the room before returning his gaze to Margery. "You know I have always admired you, Widow Turner. I know Nathaniel has not long been gone, but please consider my suit to offer you a safe and secure home." His smile exposed uneven, grey teeth as he added, "As my wife." Margery stood still as stone, unable to speak. "Widow Turner?" the tanner repeated.

Margery shook her head and swallowed her fury and horror. She addressed the unwelcome suitor, "I thank you for your kind concern and generous offer, Master Kimball. But I do not plan to remarry, either now or in the future, so please put such thoughts from your head."

The tanner looked at her, and his treacle smile transformed instantly and effortlessly into a sneering snarl, "What do you plan to do, Widow Turner?" He drew out the word "widow." "You have no home, no occupation, no family."

"Sir, that is my responsibility and my business. Please take no offense at my declination," Margery replied.

"You can scarce afford to refuse a good offer of marriage," he argued.

"Yet, that is indeed what I am doing. And now good sir, I must return to my work," Margery insisted.

"You would be a pauper, rather than the wife of a respected tradesman in good standing in this town?"

"Yes." The young woman strode across the floor and opened the door, welcoming the violently cleansing air.

"You are a fool, and a plain-faced one at that," he said. "Any woman in such a state as you find yourself would consider themselves quite fortunate to receive such an offer." The tanner spat as he rose, knocking over the mug and grabbing his cloak from the hook. "You'll be a pauper, you will." He threw the words over his shoulder as he strode, an enraged bull, out of the house. Margery closed and locked the door and thudded into a kitchen chair, her breath rasping and body shaking. *A pauper's life would be preferable to that of a beast's bride.*

EARLY SPRING

1805

Margery peeked into the keeping room on the other side of the kitchen wall. She took care not to enter this room into which she had not yet been invited. The snug space was dominated by an embroidery frame. A half-finished bed rug featuring an exuberant tree of life design in shades of malachite, carmine, and umber nestled on a black background. A pen and ink sketch and accompanying larger pattern drawn on cotton were pinned to a nearby wall. Baskets of vibrant-hued yarn rested on the floor alongside the work in progress. The young widow passed into the kitchen without setting foot into Hannah's sanctuary.

Stepping into the open hearth-ruled kitchen, Margery was assaulted by the smell of wood smoke. The tang was steeped into the very walls. Memories of the accident and Nathaniel's cruel death came flooding back. The young widow knew she could not escape the smell of smoke on a New Hampshire farm. She wondered if she would ever be able to free herself of the images that assaulted her when she encountered the scent. With difficulty, she forced her feet to move and her hands to go about the work of the morning.

Margery stepped out of the north-side kitchen door where a woodpile slumbered under the overhanging roof. She knew Agnes, even with her crutch, would not be able to accomplish this task typically assigned to the children of the house. The logs were stacked alternating in crosswise layers. Sitting alongside the pile was a basket of bark and kindling. Samuell must have had hired help for cutting, hauling with oxen sled, and splitting the wood. The harvest would have certainly come from his own woodlot, which she could see in the distance past the orchard. In the pile, she noticed primarily hickory and birch, fine burning wood for cooking and baking, with some oak and ash as well. The wood looked well-seasoned, most likely cut the previous winter. There was probably another pile, elsewhere on the farm, of this season's green wood that would be used the following year. The young widow brought in an armful to start up a fire, setting a forestick and backlog on the stone floor of the hearth, with the ash bed and kindling in the middle.

Margery stepped back outside and looked out across the unfamiliar surroundings. Beyond the dormant kitchen garden, the skeletal orchard reached its bark-sheathed fingers towards the sky. Her fingers were numb from the yet-unheated house, and she shivered despite her layers of woolen petticoats. The young widow bent to pick up a split log and suddenly something snapped inside her.

An overwhelming urge squeezed her chest and vised her head, encouraging her to take the piece of wood in her hand and smash it against the post holding up the roof. She opened her mouth in a long, silent scream. Tears coursed down her face. How could this now be her life? She had been a beloved wife. Nathaniel had sworn that they would be together forever. She was not supposed to be alone. She had entwined her very soul with his, and now she was a pauper on a stranger's farm. She closed her mouth and held her breath until she could hold it no more. Her head and heart ached, and her tears had frozen to her face.

The sound of Agnes's crutch clacking on the kitchen floor impelled Margery to shake herself and wipe her face with her apron. She reached down to fill her arms with wood and stepped back into the kitchen to begin the day. Margery knew Samuell was already in the barn and would be wanting breakfast presently. She could hear Hannah tottering around in the parlor and quickly put on a kettle for tea and stirred up the fire under the pottage that had sat in the embers throughout the night.

The young widow looked around and found pewter porringers and spoons. There was a bowl of butter frozen on a counter, and she wondered if Samuell would bring in milk. Hannah stepped into the kitchen, and Margery and Agnes turned to her with a polite, "Good morrow Mistress Wheeler."

"Not at my age, it isn't," Hannah replied. The old woman did not appear to possess a pleasant morning temperament. "Best get started on the hoecakes. Cut some bacon and fry it up as well. Samuell will be in soon," she commanded.

Not ten minutes later, the stomping of boots announced Samuell's return for breakfast. The smell of livestock preceded him as he ducked and stepped through the doorway. He turned slightly to allow for the width of his shoulders, encompassed in a well-worn waumase. Like most farmers, he favored the heavy wool shirt over the greatcoats preferred by tradesmen and others who did not work the land. He removed his felted wool work cap and placed a bucket of milk on the floor. Raising his eyes to the women and girl, he grunted "Morn."

Like mother, like son. Margery observed Samuell as he walked to the dry sink and washed his hands vigorously, then strode to the table and sat down. Hannah motioned to Margery, who quickly filled a porringer with pottage and placed it in front of the silent man. She added the hoe cakes and bacon and poured the fresh, warm milk into a jug for the table. It was a very fine breakfast.

The young widow reminded herself not to assume all farming families were hardscrabble, grimy, and unrefined. The rich farmers she had known in her hometown lived comfortable, clean lives. They hired workers to soil their hands and strain their backs. It seemed that here on the Wheeler place, Samuell was a farmer, husbandman, and orchardist who cared for his own farm, livestock, and fruit trees.

"We dine together in this house. Kitchen most days, dining room for company and holidays," Hannah pronounced. Margery and Agnes filled three more porringers and the women joined Samuell at the kitchen table.

Margery had traveled quickly through the dining room after descending the stairs earlier in the morning. A turned-leg walnut dining table and chairs sat before the fireplace, which shared a wall and chimney with the parlor. The hearth had been cold and long unlit on the dining side. A corner cupboard held plates, cups, serving dishes, and accoutrements for tea, coffee, and chocolate. A Chinese export porcelain bowl in cobalt and white with a landscape scene sat in the center place of honor.

The newcomers ate with lowered eyes. Margery considered Samuell with surreptitious glances. She saw he was a bit younger than she had imagined. Perhaps just entering his 30s. His beard was well-trimmed, and again Margery chided herself at her surprise. His hair was admittedly in need of a wash, which was not unexpected at this time of year. She noted some threads of ginger running through the auburn brown of his hair and wondered if perhaps there lay a remnant of a long-ago Scottish forbear buried in the family tree.

Samuell held himself removed and remote. So different from Nathaniel's bubbly, joyful personality. At their breakfasts in the small cottage, the young man would share his dreams, goals, and plans, some of which might have changed after a night's rest. Admittedly, it was Nathaniel doing most of the talking. Evening meals would be full of Nathaniel describing his projects and customers, often giving difficult customers unbecoming and humorous nicknames and offering rather accurate imitations. He would goad his wife into sharing what beauty she had seen in her day, as he was confined to the blacksmith shop.

Margery had learned to come to the table ready to describe the carved decorations on a neighbor's new door columns, a new litter of puppies in town, or lady slipper orchids poking their heads out of the humus on the floor of the cool damp woods. Nathaniel had deepened her ability to see. Now, she looked at Samuell's hands. They were farmer's hands, and one finger was quite crooked from a former break. But they were beautiful in their own manner. She did not feel this in a sexual way, but rather in an aesthetic appreciation.

Margery lifted her gaze and pushed Samuell's hands and the bittersweet memories of Nathaniel from her mind as Hannah called out, "Widow Turner, fill a jug with cider for Samuell to take out to the barn with him." Margery did as she was asked. She knew the farmer's cider was highly regarded in the town and that his orchard was the finest for miles around. Samuell stood from the table and lifted his bowl and spoon. He stopped and looked around the room, and then placed them back on the table.

The farmer nodded to the women and girl, turned, and went out the door, picking up the jug from the counter on his way out. Hannah made a sound that might have been a chuckle. "When it is the two of us alone and we don't have hired men and girls," she said, "Samuell cleans the dishes for me. I imagine he would prefer to not have anyone to know that." Margery brought the dishes to the dry sink.

"Can you make butter?" Hannah queried the young woman who had busied herself washing dishes.

Margery tried not to blush. "I have seen it made but have not churned myself."

"And how did you come to have butter on your table?" Hannah asked, frowning.

"At my childhood home, we always had a hired girl who worked the dairy. When I was a teacher and when I was married to Nathaniel, I had no cow and bought butter."

The old widow stood and straightened as well as she could. "Well," she said, "you'll learn today. The cows have started up their milk after calving, and we have a couple of days' milk setting out. Any simpleton can do it, but you must be calm and patient and you cannot rush."

"I am happy to learn," Margery replied in an even voice.

"I can churn," Agnes interrupted in a wee voice. "My mother said I was a good kitchen helper. But my arm gets very tired."

"We'll work as a team." Margery smiled at the wisp of a girl.

On the trip from the kitchen to the milk house, Margery looked back and observed that the original farmhouse was a two-story house with a central chimney. The single-story ell, housing a kitchen, keeping room, and pantry had been added more recently. This allowed the luxury of having a dining room and parlor on the first floor of the original structure, and separating the cooking, food preparation work, and work space from the main part of the house. Rising from the gloom of a March day and still-dormant earth, the house appeared solid and sheltering.

The morning was spent in the compact, whitewashed milk house near the barn. Hannah instructed Margery in straining milk and skimming cream off the top of the setting dishes. The cream was poured into the well-worn wooden churn. Agnes and Margery took turns patiently plunging the dasher. The girl was not much bigger than the churn and after a bit was reassigned to wash the bowls, utensils, and countertops. Hannah eventually declared they had a satisfactory ball of butter at the bottom of the churn. The buttermilk was poured off and butter placed in a cheesecloth to be squeezed dry and then rinsed. The final step, which the old woman oversaw carefully, was employing wooden paddles to salt the butter before packing it into firkins. The small wooden casks were destined to be stored in the cellar.

The women and girl did not gossip as they worked. Margery felt Hannah's eyes on her, as if gauging her temperament by how she handled the tedious task. Margery put on a pleasant and placid face and gave Hannah what she thought she was looking for. The old widow oversaw the child's cleaning tasks and enjoined, "On this farm, and especially in this milk house, we strive to heed Benjamin Franklin's words, 'Tolerate no uncleanliness in body, cloaths, or habitation.'"

Margery felt this was another "rule of the household" that was being directed at her and felt no small annoyance to have a farmer's wife instruct her so. She picked up the bucket of the buttermilk dregs and walked out of the milk house headed towards the pig trough. *Fine words, hard to heed when you are traipsing through frozen mud.*

There was no lack of chores, including the preparation of the midday dinner. The four of them sat down together for mutton stew, bread, cheese, cowcumber pickles, and apple sass. Margery had been instructed to chip a few chunks of the frozen apple sauce out of a barrel outside the door to be enjoyed after it thawed. Over dinner, Hannah requested, "Samuell, can you take these two out and show them the farm?" She continued, "Agnes, you will be in charge of feeding the chickens and collecting eggs each day. Margery, you are to take over milking the cows."

Agnes grinned and announced that she loved chickens. Margery wondered how difficult it was to milk a cow.

As the sky darkened and time for supper approached, Margery and Agnes set the table and swung the iron pot from a boiling to a warming position in the hearth. Samuell failed to appear, and eventually Hannah turned to Margery and said, "Widow Turner, bring a plate out to the barn. Samuell was expecting more troubles with the lambing."

Margery recoiled at the thought. She did not want to be in a night-darkened barn alone with a man. She looked closely into Hannah's eyes to see if they shifted in guilty knowledge about the character of her son. The old widow's brow furrowed as she saw Margery pause. The young widow turned away and prepared a covered plate. She warmed a mug of cider by plunging the toddy rod, heated red in the ashes, into the drink. She donned her cloak and set out across the dooryard and crossed over to the barn.

As she entered the barn, she was enveloped in the scent of large breathing animals. The lofty structure housed stalls for horses and cows on one side, with hay pitched on the opposite side. She crossed through the middle threshing floor and entered into an attached smaller shed where the sheep sheltered. Her appearance startled some of the flock, who moved into the dim back corners of their pens and eyed her warily, fearing danger.

Samuell was on his knees in the farthest pen, which appeared to have been set aside for the gravid ewes. The middle pen held recently-born lambs, most nursing from their mother. "Master Wheeler," she announced, "I have brought you some dinner."

"I cannot leave this little mother. Set the plate down," Samuell replied. Taking a deep breath, Samuell turned to look at Margery and said, "Widow Turner, this might not be quite appropriate to request, but I need another set of hands to see through this night's birthing. It seems as if these ewes got together and decided to all labor on the same night."

Margery faltered, then replied, "Of course, Master Wheeler," and drew nearer to the farmer.

"Please wash your hands first," the farmer requested, pointing to a wooden bucket of fresh water and a block of lye soap, probably made once a year in the fall with wood ash and the rendered fat from a freshly butchered pig. This was yet another task for Margery to look forward to mastering.

Margery had no great experience in husbandry outside of a few chickens at the smithy cottage. She could not tell if a ewe was actually in distress. The young widow felt apprehension start to squeeze her chest as she wondered if this was a ploy to get her alone. What if Master Wheeler had unpure intentions? What would she do, where would she go when she rebuffed, if she was physically able, his advances? When Nathaniel had died, Margery swore to herself that she would not take another man into her life. Would she even have a choice? The farmer was most powerfully built.

"Did you help with raising animals in the home where you grew up?" Samuell asked, interrupting her frightened thoughts.

"No, I did not, but I am not squeamish," Margery answered.

"This is the little mother's first birth. The babe's front feet are out, but her head in still inside. The lamb needs to be pushed back into the ewe's womb and have the head come out with the front legs." Samuell's voice was low and even, obviously not wanting to scare the ewe or perhaps Margery.

The farmer motioned for Margery to enter the pen and approach man and animal. "What do you need me to do?" she asked.

"Hold the mother's head and front legs and speak in a calm manner to her," the farmer requested.

Margery did as instructed, and Samuell worked on re-positioning the lamb. The young mother strained her neck and bleated piteously.

Samuell sat back. "Now we let mother and babe finish this work." The young ewe strained and shuddered with contractions. Two front legs and a nose appeared, and a perfectly shaped lamb was soon in the straw, being vigorously sniffed and licked by the first-time mother. "They are but dumb beasts, but I care not to see them suffer," he said. The farmer stood and Margery unconsciously retreated a step back.

Samuell stepped out of the birthing pen and into the adjoining pen with mothers and their new lambs. He turned to Margery and said, "Ah, this mother had three babes this morning, but has stopped feeding one of them. What I would ask you to do is bring the wee rejected one and see if this other mother, who had one living lamb and one stillborn, will accept this one as a second babe, and allow him to nurse." He continued, "I need to wrap up a broken leg on one of the babes. I think he got stepped on by one of the mothers."

Margery sidled past Samuell and entered the pen. She picked up the small creature, who was sitting by himself rather than standing and feeding like the other little ones. For a moment, Margery reveled in the perfectness of the tiny creature and felt the fluttering of its heart under her fingers.

She knelt slowly in the straw, positioning herself to be facing the stall gate, to better keep an eye on Samuell. She tried not to startle the mother with the single lamb. She stood the rejected lamb on his wobbly legs next to the udders of the mother. Samuell had crutched the dirty wool from around the ewe's udder to assist the newborn lambs in finding the mother's distended teats. The ewe allowed the little foster lamb to nurse, and Samuell smiled at them from his task across the room.

Margery felt a sense of satisfaction and smiled back at the farmer. "There's no certainty she will accept the little one permanently, but it's a good sign," Samuell said. His eyes were red and weary, but he carried an indefatigable air as he gazed at his flock. "I think things are under control here now and you can return to the house." His eyes were sweeping over the livestock as he added, "I thank you for your assistance and for supper."

"Of course, I am happy to help," Margery said as she stood and wiped her hands on her apron and turned to return to the house. She felt relief and a small, rather small, flicker of joy from witnessing the new life so recently come into the world.

When Margery was finally able to crawl into bed next to a slumbering Agnes, she was exhausted in body and mind.

She had worked tirelessly and without complaint. She was grateful that Hannah and Samuell, while stern-faced, were not cruel and asked no more from her than they asked of themselves. She knew she was safe. She knew she would be fed and have a roof over her head. This was a life, but so different from her life as she had known it with Nathaniel. She allowed herself to indulge in the heartsickness and despair that visited her when her hands and mind were idle. She attempted to rally herself with a promise. *This is how I am existing now, but I will create a life for myself.*

She looked at the sleeping child beside her and felt a flicker of shame. This young one had lived such a short time before the tragic loss of her mother. Margery had not until this moment realized that throughout the day, the quiet girl had diligently undertaken her chores in this new home. Agnes neither complained nor carried a surly expression. Margery didn't think she had even smiled at the girl once throughout the day, too wrapped up in her own self-pity. Agnes had probably never spent time away from her home before, and now she was without kin among strangers. Margery vowed to raise herself above her own misery and offer some small comforts to the grieving girl. She found that thinking on how to ease the child's sorrow lifted her away from her own, if only for a little while.

As Odysseus yearned for his apple orchards as he made his way home to Ithaca, Samuell waited on the snows of winter to recede so he could return to his orchard. The day had broken brilliant, a gift to the winter-worn farmers and townspeople alike. Over breakfast, Samuell announced he was to work on winter pruning of the apple trees in the hillside orchard. It was a bit late in the season to be just beginning this task. But last year's winter snows had come early and had continued with a series of storms and nor'easters into the months of the new year.

He departed with a light step, leaving the women to the dim interior of the kitchen. The orchardist returned for an early midday dinner, the cold shedding off him, causing Margery to shiver. Distracted and mute, he acted as if his mind and heart were still in the orchard, while his body took life-giving sustenance from the well-laden table and warmth from the substantial fire in the hearth.

Midafternoon, Margery looked out the window and observed that the morning sapphire sky had disappeared and grey clouds now scudded across the firmament. She spoke up, "Mistress Wheeler, would you like me to bring Master Wheeler some warm cider, as the weather seems to be turning?"

"I suppose we don't want to have to dig him out of that orchard half-frozen," Hannah opined.

Margery warmed the cider and filled a jug with the clear, lightly alcoholic liquid, then bundled up to walk to the orchard.

Samuell saw Margery's approach and put down his tools with ill-hidden regret. He accepted the jug and took a long draught. He sighed in appreciation. Margery looked at the litter of cut branches around the trees. Many of the pruned branches looked healthy, and she wondered about the calculations made for rejecting boughs.

Seeming to glean her thoughts, Samuell said, "It is not just broken or diseased limbs that must be removed for a tree to grow hale and fruitful." He pointed to the tree he had been working on. "Branches are cut to let in light and air, and permit the energy of the tree to flow into the limbs that remain."

He pointed to a smooth, young branch extending skyward from a thicker gnarled one with many spurs. "This branch looks hale enough," he said, "but when you look closely at it, it has no buds that will become apples. It is not productive wood and needs to be removed." He paused and ran his hand along the older, unlovely branch and continued, "This branch might not be pleasing to the eye, but see how it extends outward, rather than upward. Trees whose branches grow out rather than up can bend, rather than breaking under the great weight of snow and ice."

Margery nodded and made a hum of acknowledgement as she looked at the trees with a new appreciation. "'Tis a discerning eye that is needed, I now see. Did your father teach you how be an orchardist?"

"Aye, he taught me many things about caring for trees and the making of cider. Did you know that the Mayflower ship carried apple trees, seeds, and apples to this shore, along with the English passengers?"

"No, I guess I did not," Margery replied. "Your trees give us cider to drink, pippins to eat, and vinegar to preserve our summer bounty. They are most valuable," she added.

"Indeed, they are," Samuell said and he might have smiled.

The young widow noted that the orchardist's natural reserve melted away when he spoke of his trees. She saw his love of this place in his eyes, and it reminded her of the enjoyment Nathaniel took from crafting in iron. She had seen that look in her blacksmith husband's eyes when he showed her the everyday objects he decorated with flourishes imitating nature, such as scrolls of vines or ferns, leaves, and flowers. He would solicit her for the drawings she would make when she walked in the fields and woods, and use them as inspiration for his work.

"We are partners, you and I, my love," he'd said. "Your art is in my metal."

"Well, I don't think Farmer Peterson will appreciate any iron flowers on his harrow you are mending," Margery had teased.

"Aye, but I would dearly love to see his face when I handed a pretty harrow back to him."

"And I would like you to continue to be the town's blacksmith and allow us to put food on the table," Margery said, only half joking.

Margery picked up a pruned twig and spun it. Samuell continued, "The discarded branches have a role to play too. After they are collected and dried, they will be used in the smokehouse for the hams. Their smoke is most sweet."

"Well, that is very practical," Margery noted.

"Indeed. Thank you for the cider," Samuell replied, and abruptly turned his attention back to the trees.

Margery retreated down the hill back to the farmhouse, sloshing through the slush that refused to acknowledge spring's return. On her way, she picked up a handful of pruned apple branches, running her fingers along both the twisted, rough and straight, smooth wood and envisioning how she would sketch them when she had a few minutes free today. She wondered if she would ever find her natural gift that would both fulfill her and allow her to support herself while creating something of use and beauty. She would not forever remain a pauper in purse or in purpose.

Margery caressed the ice-cold iron thumb latch as she opened the door to the kitchen. She pictured Nathaniel's hammer gripped in his hand, rising up, then striking the malleable metal. "Did everything go alright with Samuell?" Hannah queried.

"Oh, yes, fine. I was just lost in memories for a moment." Margery lifted the corners of her mouth.

"I do well know how that happens," Hannah said softly. The old woman shook her head and regained her gruff demeanor. "Widow Turner, as you can see, Samuell will not leave the orchard until he is satisfied with his pruning. It will be days, if not a fortnight. I need you to go to town to pick up supplies and the post at Stanton's."

The younger woman blanched. "I'm...I'm not ready to go to town. I can't."

Hannah's voice was firm. "You cannot hide on this farm forever," she said. "There is no reason you should be ashamed to show your face in town. You are a widow without a mite by no fault of your own. Why, if you think of the sins and secrets many of the folk in this town hold close, it is they who should avoid the eyes of their fellow townsmen." The old woman continued, "And we are running out of meal and salt. Samuell needs nails." Hannah cleared her throat and looked down as she realized the effect the last item would have on Margery. She went on, "I have some crocks of apple butter still that I wanted to trade for maple syrup. The sap has just about finished its run. And maybe a few pins. But more importantly, I am expecting a letter from my daughter."

Margery swallowed the anguish that rose at the mention of the blacksmith goods, now brought in from the nearby town of Farringham. Thorneboro had not yet found a new blacksmith for their own. "You have a daughter?" Margery asked in surprise.

"I do." Hannah's reply included no elaboration.

After this admission, Margery could not find it in her heart to refuse the old widow and agreed to set off to Stanton's in the morning with Hannah's list.

Persephone, as her name implied, was the gentler of the two horses. Demeter, like her Greek goddess namesake, stamped her feet and shook her head in distress as she observed Samuell hitch her daughter up to a smaller cart than the one he typically drove. The farmer had sullenly resented even the few minutes it took for this chore that kept him from his orchard. Persephone, unlike the devoted and ever-homesick daughter of the myth, remained placid in the face of the adventure that lay before her.

Samuell handed Margery up into the cart and loaded a wooden box. Inside, the crocks of apple butter were nestled amongst straw used to protect them during the journey over the rough early spring road. Conscious of Samuell watching to see how she handled the wain, Margery clucked her tongue, and Persephone cooperatively walked across the dooryard and into the lane headed to town. Margery, rather than Persephone, felt as if she were the one unwillingly journeying into the underworld.

The town sniffed haughtily as Margery guided Persephone past the preening homes of those who did not toil on farms. Even those who were only one generation past a hardscrabble English croft seemed to conveniently forget their humble heritages, and took great pleasure in their elevated positions on the social ladder of the town. She passed Henry Marsh's cooperage. The cooper had depended on Nathaniel's forged-iron hoops for his oak barrels, and the two men had often enjoyed a pipe and a mug of ale as they transacted business.

Today, the doors of the cooper's shop were flung open, and the craftsman was working in the weak morning sunshine. He lifted his head, registering surprise at the sight of Margery. Clearing her throat she offered, "Good morrow, Master Marsh." He nodded without rising, his eyes quickly lowering as he recognized the widow. Her back stiffened in surprise and sorrow at the muted greeting. She remembered the look of gratitude on his face when she had brought warm dinners to his family as his oldest child suffered and ultimately perished from consumption.

The young widow shook her shoulders and continued on, now mutely nodding at passersby rather than attempting greeting. Most returned her nod. Others found reason to look away. She pulled up in front of Stanton's General Store and tied Persephone up to the hitching rail. She walked to the back of the cart to retrieve the goods to be traded.

During her marriage, Margery had entered this store hundreds of times. Margery always hoped to encounter Mr. Stanton rather than his shrew of a wife. She was happy enough just looking at the new fabrics or teapots, not tempted to buy inessentials, unlike her profligate husband. Her occasional treat might be a handful of molasses drops added to her foodstuff purchases.

When Margery had rented a room under the Stanton's roof and assisted in the shop, she had observed the less-than-ethical practices of Mrs. Stanton. Adding decayed potatoes or onions better fit for hogs to the bottom of a barrel sold to an elderly shopper. A thumb on the scale measuring out tea or tobacco when a housewife sent in her child to pick up an order. The shopmistress knew who could be cheated and who could not. Assuming avarice lived in the hearts of all, Mrs. Stanton had watched Margery like a hawk.

The young widow paused and looked at the closed doors of the shop with trepidation. Her face was already burning in...what? Shame? Fury? Desolation? Margery mounted the stairs and entered the store. Mrs. Stanton's feigned smile with which she greeted customers disappeared as she turned and saw the young widow cross the threshold.

"Miss Turner," she said. So it began. The term "Miss" was reserved for young unmarried women. When used to address a married woman, it was an old form of address that could mean "prostitute." If the shopmistress had used the word in error, she did not correct herself.

Margery turned her head at a sound towards the back of the shop. Rebecca Dean, wife of Bennett Dean, the cabinetmaker, had placed down the ribbon she had been examining and walked towards the door, calling out, "I shall return at another time." She walked by Margery as if the young widow was an underworld shade. Mrs. Stanton glared at Margery, the cause of a lost or at least postponed sale.

"And what takes you away from your master today?" The shopmistress said, her sneer curdling her already-unlovely face.

Margery wondered what she could have done to earn this woman's enmity. "I have a list from Mistress Wheeler and have two crocks of apple butter to trade for maple syrup, if you have it. I was also asked to collect the post." Mrs. Stanton took the list with a harrumph and without another word turned to begin filling the order.

As Margery walked around the shop, she passed the barrel of square nails, hand-forged by an unknown blacksmith. Perhaps he had a wife and children and returned smoky and soot-covered to their loving embraces at the end of each day. She moved on and stopped in front of a hooded cloak cut from a felted wool of rich burgundy. She rubbed the material appreciatively and admired the pewter clasp fastened at the neckline. Mrs. Stanton declared,

"Mistress Wheeler surely won't pay for such finery as you've been accustomed to. Please don't touch the garments, unless, that is, Master Wheeler has promised you some pretty things for your services."

The shopmistress's voice dripped with venom, and Margery could not continue to ignore the woman's incivility. She spun around towards the counter with eyes blazing and said, "Why do you torment me and treat me with such disrespect? I lost my husband, my home, and my freedom. Do you believe I deserve this most unfortunate of fates? I am a pauper, not a whore."

Mrs. Stanton was taken aback for a beat before her own eyes narrowed and her voice rose, "You have no right to fall upon the town and our coffers. You were not born here. Your husband was not born here. You have brought forward no children from your union that would rightfully be citizens of this town. You should have been warned out." The shopmistress stopped to wipe the spittle off her chin. She went on, "Now, you have set your eyes on Samuell Wheeler, a man who should marry a young woman born and bred of Thorneboro. Everyone in the town feels this way."

Margery sputtered, "The townsmen deemed me eligible for relief. Do you think that this is what I dreamed of for myself? My husband dead, my home gone. No kin or family. I have not set my sights on Master Wheeler and I have no plans to take a husband, or a lover." She took a breath and attempted to regain her composure. "I complete the duties set before me at the Wheeler Farm to the best of my abilities and I am grateful to be taken in."

"I'm sure you complete your duties," the shopmistress replied, drawing out the last word before continuing, "with much enthusiasm."

Margery realized that there was no changing the mind, or heart, of the sanctimonious woman standing in front of her. "Is the Wheeler order complete?"

"It is all here, added to the Wheeler account," the shopmistress said, emphasizing the name of Margery's sponsors.

"And the post?" Margery enquired.

"Nothing," Mrs. Stanton replied airily.

Margery doubted the woman's word on this, but she had no recourse and turned to escape the ordeal. She exited the store, unhitched Persephone, and mounted the cart seat. A pair of boys, who should have been in school, field, or a tradeshop, rolled dice along the side of the store. They stopped to stare at Margery, silent, with mouths agape. A pauper sighting to pass along to family and friends. Margery urged Persephone into an unaccustomed trot, and she found herself desperate to be back on the farm.

Margery kept her eyes on the dough she was kneading in a wooden trencher. Hannah was keeping a side eye on the younger woman's technique while she herself rolled out pie crusts. Agnes was assigned to soaking and chopping dried pumpkin slices for a pie. It was Saturday. Baking day on the Wheeler Farm, as it was for most rural households. For those with large families, a mid-week baking day was also required. Cooking on Saturday might have allowed women a bit of a reprieve on Sunday, but they were required to spend their "day of rest" attending the all-day Sabbath services at the meetinghouse.

The young widow had risen before dawn and lit a fire in the brick beehive oven adjacent to the open hearth. After a few hours, the fire had burned down to coal, the bread had risen on the sideboard, and it was time to bake. The bread in the Wheeler household was primarily rye 'n injun, a combination of rye flour and Indian cornmeal, although Hannah occasionally traded apple vinegar or boiled cider for wheat flour from Stanton's. The yeast in the dough came from beer barrel dregs that had been traded for with a neighbor. The Wheelers primarily drank the hard cider they produced themselves, rather than ale or small beer.

While she could often peacefully clear her mind as she completed the long-memorized baking day tasks, today Margery found her mind revisiting memories as her hands remained busy. In particular, the kneading of the dough reminded her of Nathaniel's playful threats when he entered the kitchen at dinnertime on a baking day, to "offer his help." Approaching her from behind as she was working the dough in the trough, he would extend his sooty hands around and past her waist and threaten to plunge them into the pristine dough. Some days, like today, her entire life with Nathaniel, those few, perfect years, spooled through her head. She silently reeled between biting her tongue in laughter, remembering his silly antics, and shedding scalding tears into the dough.

Margery shoved the embers out of the oven and wiped it down with a wet sorghum broom. She tossed a handful of cornmeal onto the oven floor to gauge the temperature by watching how it browned. She preferred that technique to the one used by some women who would calculate the temperature by thrusting their bare arms into the oven and counting how long they could bear the heat. Five seconds meant the oven was too hot, while fifteen seconds was considered too cool for baking.

She placed the bread in the oven and inserted the heavy wooden door into the opening. As the day progressed, the women baked mince, pumpion, and chicken pie, gingerbread, squash pudding, and apple custard. When the baked goods were done, Margery would place a pot of beans and salt pork in boiled cider into the back of the oven to cook overnight.

Come midmorning of working side by side, Hannah's silence broke. "It was a great loss, the blacksmith, your husband," she said. Margery startled at both the voice and the sentiment, then nodded in the direction of the old woman. Hannah continued, "My Ezekiel passed some twenty years ago. He was one of the few who came home safely after serving in Washington's army." Margery heard the note of pride in the old widow's voice. "He had but lost a few toes to frostbite. Ezekiel even avoided the scourge of the smallpox that was in all the colonies and among the troops, both British and Continental." She paused as she recalled the story. "Commander Washington put smallpox from the plagued into cuts made on the arms of 40,000 soldiers, my Ezekiel being one of them. None in the colonies nor the British knew of Washington's plan to fight that invisible enemy. My husband swore that Washington's trick helped the Continental Army win the war."

Margery had seen smallpox victims and the disgusting pustules that covered their skin. She couldn't imagine putting the pus into a cut on a healthy person's arm. Her stomach clenched. Hannah read her mind. "Yes, it sounds a horror, but all I know is that Ezekiel came home to his family and his precious farm." Margery smiled and thought of how Samuell now loved the homestead as his father once had. Hannah continued, "He expanded the orchard and replaced the small cider mill with one big enough to serve as cider mill to the town – selling his own products and allowing town residents to bring their crops in for cider-making as well."

"What befell your husband, then?" Margery finally asked. She looked into Hannah's faded, cornflower-blue eyes.

"Ezekiel dropped dead in that orchard some four years after returning from war. 'Tis an irony. He was found by Samuell when he did not return for supper. Felled by his heart, Midwife Bradford thought."

The women worked in silence for a few minutes before Margery asked a second question. "Do you have living children besides Samuell? You mentioned a daughter."

Hannah pursed her lips as she looked over at the younger woman. "Aye," she said. "I have three living children. The girl, Beatrice, is married out and has two bairns, both boys, with another child on the way. She married her school sweetheart and they moved to Western New York. I expected the post to carry a letter from her about the birth." Hannah's face looked both wistful and worried.

She went on, "My second-eldest, Simon, left the farm and became a minister. He has a parish in Keene. He always hated to toil in the dirt, preferring books and such. Samuell is the one who loves the farm. He can't bear to be away from it. It runs in his blood." Hannah looked towards the window. The small slate headstones in the graveyard atop the hill were not visible from where she sat, but she could see them clearly. "There were two babes who did not survive," Hannah said simply.

"I am much aggrieved to hear that," Margery offered. The two women fell into silence, each remembering loves and losses.

Stepping out of the hearth-ruled kitchen was like throwing off a comforting unwashed quilt. In the bright, brittle sunlight, Margery felt a stirring in her heart. From the stoop, she saw the frost retreating along the path of the sunbeams. A single amethyst crocus reached out from alongside the foundation, with sisters soon to follow. The west side of the fence posts was hoary with ice crystals, while those on the east side dripped and glistened with melted water. The roof of the barn released wreaths of steam. Tufts of grasses interspersed with clumps of bluets sprouted in the pasture. No heart could be so hardened that it did not leap at the glorious beginning of such a day.

Margery visited the necessary and then turned to walk towards the orchard with her foraging basket in hand and her knife around her neck. When she went out hunting for wild edibles, she took the walnut-handled foraging knife Nathaniel had crafted for her forays. It was similar to the small patch knives most men carried. As with the men's knives, Margery's blade was stored and carried around her neck. Nathaniel had traded for the tooled-leather sheath and cord with Peterson, the leather-worker in town. This was one of the small handful of gifts from Nathaniel that Margery had been able to retain.

While the apple blossoms still slept in tight buds, white snowdrops nodded from emerald stems carpeting the ground under the orchard trees. Some emerged from snow still lying in the shade of the trees. At the edge of the woods, the praying hand bushes were opening to present bouquets of white five-petaled flowers. These clever hobblebushes were one of the first forest residents to leaf and flower, while their taller brethren of beech, maple, oak, chestnut, and birch were more fickle and required more than a promise of warmth. The hopeful clusters signaled bees were soon to emerge from their straw skeps to forage after their cozy winter, enjoying any hard-earned honey the farmers didn't steal. Margery promised to herself to find joy from the magnificence of nature on this day, rather than focus on the drudgery that was a great part of a day on a farm.

Although not responsible for farm tasks such as husbandry while she was growing up, Margery had been trained by her mother in some of the food arts, including the collecting of wild edibles from the forest. Margery thought of her mother as she stepped into the cool embrace of the woods and took a deep breath. She did not know these new woods and wondered if she could find a patch of pungent ramps, the evasive wild leeks that grew only in the deep forest. Fried in bacon fat, they would be a welcome first fresh vegetable of the season after the long monochromatic, winter menu.

Her mother had taught her that the Abenaki, who lived here long before settlers, called these plants *Winooski*. Margery knew to look in the moist undergrowth under canopy of a hardwood forest, preferably on a cool north slope. Margery also knew the difference between ramps and their poisonous twin, false hellebore, which did not bear the same powerful oniony smell. In a few weeks, these woods would be enclosed in dense shade. Other spring ephemerals such as ginseng, mayapple, and trout lily needed to soak up the weak sunshine before they fell into summer shade. As the young woman stepped into the forest, she felt welcomed as if by an old friend.

The pungent scent of lanolin preceded Samuell as he came into the kitchen for midday dinner. He was accompanied by Hiram Broadbent, who was known in town for his skill with sheep shears. The animals had been divested of their coats today. Hiram greeted the women and girl politely and cast his eyes around, examining every inch of the space. Throughout the meal, which did indeed feature the precious ramps, Margery felt as if under a magnifying glass. Hiram's eyes never stopped tracking every movement and every word out of the mouths of those sitting at the dinner table. Was he searching for evidence that there was any impropriety in Margery's presence at the farm? She had been at the farm for five weeks and knew the inevitable gossip that had floated around since the town meeting. Many thought that Samuell had brought her to the farm for more than household help. Hiram Broadbent would have no titillating stories to report back on his next visit to Allen's Tavern.

Oxen shoes clinked on loose stones in the distance. Margery lifted her head to watch the beast, cart, and man draw closer. She continued to work in the kitchen garden, planting pole beans until the pair stopped in front of the farm. A willowy man climbed down from the wagon and approached the young widow. The wagon held an odd wooden sled, flat with no sides. She knew it to be a stone scow. But the man was what drew her complete attention. Life on a farm was not kind to those who toiled to pull sustenance out of the rocky soil. It aged man and woman so they appeared wrinkled and wizened before their time.

This stranger's face was unlined and radiant with health, featuring deep-set brown eyes. His black hair was long and hung loose down his back. His clothes were ill-fitting and none too clean. His hands were long and slender, though his fingernails were jagged. His hands looked much older than his face. He was surely a man who made a living with his hands. She guessed him to be out of his youth, but still a young man. A black, white, and grey dog of indeterminate breed jumped down to join the man. Despite the animal's obvious eagerness to explore the new surroundings and the many intriguing smells, he remained at the man's side.

Margery stood and wiped her hands on her apron, keeping her eyes trained on the unexpected visitor.

"Mistress, I did not mean to startle you," the man said. "I am seeking the master of the house to enquire if he might be in need of a stonemason to build him stone walls. I do also know well animals, farms, and orchards, and can swing an axe all of the day." The traveler spoke in English with a French lilt.

"I am but help myself," she replied. "The master will be in the orchard and you are welcome to find him. Indeed, we may be able to use another hand around here."

"I thank you Mistress," the stranger said, inclining his head. He turned and strode towards the tree-studded hill.

When Samuell entered the kitchen for midday dinner, the stranger accompanied him. Margery had told Hannah and Agnes of the stranger's arrival.

Samuell announced, "Mother, Margery, Agnes, this is Joseph Fisher. He is going to stay on to turn our many piles of stone into some fine walls, beginning with some around the pastures. He will help with the harvest and cidering, too."

Hannah squinted her eyes at the man and bluntly enquired, "Are you an Indian?"

A few uneasy moments of silence hovered before Joseph replied, "Mistress, my people are *Alnôbak*. 'People of the Dawn' in your language. I come from a village along the Saint-François River, near Montréal." Silence once again patiently looked around the room.

"Well, that is a considerable way to travel to build a wall," Hannah harrumphed. The old woman paused and added, "We shall see." She turned to Margery with pursed lips, "Set another plate."

During the meal, Margery stole glances at Joseph. She was curious to see if he ate as a civilized man or as a savage. He partook of the dinner in the same manner as the rest of them, and certainly presented himself as more civilized than some white men she had seen in the tavern. Agnes was not so subtle and stared openly at Joseph with her mouth agape.

Hannah chided, "we don't all need to see your dinner as it sits in your mouth, young lady. Chew with your mouth closed or you can take your meal with the other cows in the pasture."

"But I have never seen an Indian before," Agnes argued. She ate with her mouth closed for a few minutes and looked up again. "What is your dog's name?" Agnes asked.

"*Azeban* is his name. It is the name of a raccoon trickster in my people's stories."

"He's not welcome here if he bothers the livestock," Hannah announced.

"Oh no, Mistress, he is a ratter and will be of great help in the barn. His mother was an Injun dog, but his father was an Irish terrier belonging to an Irish fur trader."

"We'll see," Hannah said, giving more attention than needed on buttering a crumbling piece of cornbread.

Joseph continued to look at Agnes, "My ox has a name as well," he said. "It is *Mahom*. It means 'Grandfather.'"

"Is he so very old?" Agnes queried.

"He is old, but he is strong."

Silence settled over the table and the stranger did not speak or raise his eyes again during the meal. When the dinner was over, he quietly thanked the women and followed Samuell back out the door.

"There are some who would not have an Indian under their roof," Hannah muttered. "But this is Samuell's farm and he is tasked with who lives and works here."

Margery reflected on the fact that this native man was free to hire himself out, earn money, and leave if he desired, but she was a pauper who had been bought, rather than having chosen her place. She tried to shake away the thoughts and reminded herself that this family had treated her well.

The following day, Joseph began his labors. Samuell wanted to see proof of the stonemason's skill before he wrote up a contract. The two men had walked the boundary lines around the farm and between pastures and fields, discussing the routes of the proposed walls after supper the previous evening. The men and boys of the Wheeler family had been clearing fields since they had acquired the land. As they cleared more and more land each year, the

Wheeler farmers had been hauling sleds of granite fieldstone, dumping them on the outer edges of pastures and the borders of tilled fields and forest.

Timber split-rail fencing, called "zig-zag fencing" by some, had been erected to divide fields separating animals and crops. While effective, wooden fences rotted over time and needed repair and replacement. Wooden rails had a short lifespan in the harsh New England climate.

What Joseph was tasked to do was to build double stone walls, two parallel rows of stone with a center gap filled with smaller stones. Such walls were typically the height of a man's thigh, and those to be used to keep in or keep out foraging animals needed to have wooden rails added to the top to reach the height required by the town fence viewer. In addition to the stone scow, Joseph had brought the tools of a stonemason – hammers, chisels and points, shovel, pry bar, pickaxe, string, chain, and thick leather gloves.

After a few days, Samuell examined the few feet of stacked wall completed by Joseph and declared it handsome and strong. He argued with Hannah that a fine stone wall would stand without tumbling for generations, and received back a grunt in reply. Margery caught Hannah looking out the kitchen window towards the fragment of the wall and she had the impression that Hannah might be secretly pleased at the prospect of such a fine addition to the farm. That night, after dinner, Samuell wrote a contract by tallow candlelight at the kitchen table.

On the 4th day of June in the Year of our Lord one thousand eight hundred and aught five, Samuell Wheeler does enter into agreement with Joseph Fisher to Dig and Haul stones and make a fine stone wall for a fence the length of approximately 48 rods and four-and-a-half-foot tall. The facing stones shall be no smaller than two-handed stones. The said Samuell Wheeler will comfort with good and sufficient meat, drink, and lodging for the term of not more than one year and 120 dollars upon completion.

Witness our hands & seals
The day and year above-mentioned.

Both men signed and sealed the record, and it was placed in Samuell's wooden document box, kept atop a chest of drawers in his bedroom.

Some days were better than others and today the day smelled like Margery felt. The smell of manure snuck into the house, permeating rooms, clothing, bedding. *I might as well be living at the bottom of the privy,* Margery griped to no one but herself as she headed to the barn to milk the cows. Before Joseph had made too much progress on the wall, he had been called by Samuell to help with preparing the fields for planting. Perhaps the most disagreeable of farm tasks, wagonloads of manure, collected over the winter, had to be spread on the fields as they were plowed and harrowed. An ever-present coating of mud and manure encased farmer, equipment, and floors.

Later in the day, as Margery hung out the washing, she observed a rabble of yellow and black swallowtail butterflies settle on a pile of manure that had bumped off the cart. This image did nothing to lighten her mood. Margery had been up before dawn, filling the kettle with water and lighting a fire underneath before boiling, scrubbing, rinsing, and wringing the laundry. Her hands stung from the caustic lye soap.

She was also still irked that she had lost an entire bucket of milk that morning, kicked over by a hoof just as she had finished filling the pail. She had not become comfortable or agile in milking. She was sure that the cows were exquisitely aware of this fact and actively contributed to her difficulties. They seemed to take pains to shuffle their feet, causing streams of milk to veer onto the floor rather than the bucket. Samuell had observed her one morning, shaking his head and mumbling, not unkindly, about how he had never seen one as inept as she was in this simple task that had been done by farmers for generations.

Margery saw that in addition to hauling manure to the fields being plowed by Samuell and Demeter and Persephone, Joseph was also picking and pulling rocks loosened by the plow from the fields. He piled them on his stone boat to be dragged to the next section of wall to be completed. Unlike the orchard, which needed no plowing and could be planted around tree stumps and stone, a field for corn, rye grass, potatoes, and other crops needed to be tamed. No matter how many times a New England field is plowed, a spring crop of devil's teeth emerges from the ground, perennially heaved up to the surface by frost. Picking rocks is a fact of life on a farm, and there was no use complaining about it. The thrifty New England farmer took the bedeviling stone harvest and reclaimed it to form the practical work of art that is the stone wall.

EARLY SUMMER
1805

The weather begins to be more settled.

~ Leavitt's Farmer's Almanac, 1805

Early summer teased as the plowed and harrowed fields began to dry. The frosts had finally ceased. As the weather warmed, the men had exchanged their wool work caps for straw ones. They wore linen workshirts and trousers. Samuell's feet were shod in simple leather shoes, while Joseph preferred moccasins.

The road down the hill to the center of Thorneboro had been troughs of mud for the past few weeks. Impossible to navigate during mud season, it had finally hardened up, allowing the hill farmers to take horse and wagon to town. Hay was the first major crop to be harvested and required every hand on the farm for a few weeks. Day laborers made their way between the scattered farms. The corn looked to be knee-high by the fourth of July, promising a fine yield come late summer.

The women had finished planting the kitchen garden and were adding the welcome green of garden peas and chives, as well as foraged dandelion leaves and purslane, to dishes. Hannah had a spring to her step, or as much of a spring as her swollen knees would allow. She had finally received a letter from her daughter, sharing the news that her family had grown by one strong and bonny little girl. Beatrice's first daughter. The child had been named Hannah Charlotte.

Agnes was blooming as well. Her stick-thin body was becoming more substantial. Her face had lost the hungry gauntness it had worn when she first arrived at the farm. Margery noticed that the girl never spoke of her family or the tragedies that had befallen them. Perhaps Agnes was tamping down the painful memories. Perhaps Agnes knew, even in her young heart, that life was cruel to most and sorrow was common and not exclusive. Perhaps Agnes was practical and setting her mind single-handedly toward living in the moment and taking advantage of her current fortunate circumstance. Did it have to be only one of those reasons? Of course not. Humans were complicated.

America's Independence Day was celebrated in grand fashion in Thorneboro, as in other towns throughout the Great Republic. Ministers, tradesmen, farmers, and apprentices alike were all given the time to join the nationalistic celebration of their membership in the fledgling nation and the sacrifices made to achieve it. The residents of Wheeler Farm were no exception. It was the 29th birthday of the United States of America. A rare day of ease for a farmer in July.

Margery begged to stay home from the festivities of the day. "Someone needs to stay home and take care of the animals," she argued.

"Joseph has everything well under control," Hannah retorted with a frown.

"Please, can you understand that I don't feel comfortable when I'm in town?" The young widow swallowed her pride and begged.

"You cannot hide forever," Hannah said firmly. "Besides, Agnes and I will need help getting around."

With that reproach, Margery hung her head and returned to the house to change into her best summer frock.

As Samuell drove the wagon into town, typically taciturn fellows cheerfully raised their hands in welcome, having started their celebrations at the tavern early. "The town looks so pretty," Agnes said, her head swiveling from side to side as she tried not to miss a single sight.

"As do you, my dear," Hannah said with uncharacteristic kindness.

Earlier in the morning, the old widow had braided strips of red, white, and blue cloth into Agnes's braid. Margery had been directed to weave the same cloth into the manes and tails of Demeter and Persephone. Four of the five residents of Wheeler Farm were wearing their Sunday finest and now were sweating patriotically in the broiling summer sun.

The Thorneboro Meetinghouse doors had donned flag bunting, and the front doors were flung open in welcome. The schoolchildren had crafted public-spirited banners, which now hung from the buttonball tree sitting in front of the building. Politicians and minister shared the pulpit for a program featuring paeans to the wisdom of Washington and reminders that Continental soldiers had fought for God's own cause. Town leaders intoxicated on draughts of justice, liberty, and prosperity exalted the memory of a revolution that had swept away the bonds of a monarchical oppressor. They called to all in booming voices to rejoice in the shared inheritance of independence.

The procession of red-faced, proud men reminded the townspeople of the duties incumbent upon them and warned liberty was a fragile thing to be guarded and defended. Altogether there were more than a dozen speeches, ranging in subject from the heroism of George Washington to the importance of supporting Thorneboro's farmers. Nor were women forgotten, as the acknowledgements included recognition of their role in raising the virtuous young Americans who would be the future's leaders. When the slate of sermons and orations concluded, the Declaration of Independence, that sacred secular text, was read. Upon completion, the minister dismissed the allegiant attendees towards the town green to celebrate with the simple pleasures of games, visiting, and picnicking.

Older children and young unmarried men and women enjoyed sack and relay races. Younger ones shrieked as they enjoyed games of Duck, Duck, Goose, and Fox and Chickens. Graces was played with airborne ribbon-bedecked hoops. Larger hoops were trundled along with the help of wooden dowels. The goal was to keep the hoop upright for the longest period of time. Competition was not relegated to games or children and young adults. Women surreptitiously examined each other's pies for visible flaws and tasted them with smiles and praise, while judging darkly in their hearts. Girls on the cusp of adulthood accepted and rejected the attentions of the gawky young men and some older gents as well.

As Margery stood on the edge of the green watching Agnes sit on the sidelines of the races, she felt a cold sense of unease. She looked up and saw the tanner, Jacob Kimball, tankard in hand, staring balefully at her from across the green. Looking away quickly, she strode to the table, where Hannah and some older townswomen were debating signs that might portend that the minister's wife was expecting another child. She joined the women, but not the conversation. Her eyes roamed the crowd for Samuell and found him deep in discussion with some of his farming neighbors. No doubt comparing the progress of crops this year with years past. Unlike the other men, spry and bent alike, scattered across the common, he never seemed to rake his eyes over or even glance at the women or girls all competing to be seen.

The afternoon featured a parade where the women waved handkerchiefs. The men, many now far into their cups, cheered and shouted. The evening closed with bells rung, guns fired, music and dancing, and fireworks. There were memorable, if not skillful, first kisses in the shadows, and broken-hearted tears shed into damp, embroidered handkerchiefs.

In previous years, Margery had watched the fireworks while lying on a blanket with her head on Nathaniel's lap, her face towards the heavens. Now she wondered if Nathaniel could see the fireworks from the other side of where she now sat. The shawl she had wrapped herself in against the cool night was no substitute for her husband's warm embrace.

At the end of the festivities, Samuell had to lift and carry the sleeping Agnes from the blanket where she had nodded off. Margery helped a limping Hannah to the carriage. The draft horses, unperturbed by the merrymaking townspeople, the illuminated sky, or the explosions of the fireworks, carried the group home. After all were abed and candles extinguished, Margery gave in to her grief. In the morning, her pillow was still damp and her heart still ached.

The holiday pleasures of river-cooled watermelon, cakes, unhurried conversation, and the lively music, games, and dancing fast became a memory, as the back-breaking toil of summer farming resumed. But all pleasure was not forsworn. Summer evenings on a farm gifted long hours of golden light that were sorely missed in the other New England seasons. Most of those hours were taken up with the unending chores of the bountiful growing season on a farm. Others were stolen for moments of relaxation, although even in these moments, hands were seldom idle. Rough-worn clothes needed mending and tools needed sharpening, even when one was sitting under a tree after dinner.

More than once, Azeban trotted over and proudly laid a dead barn rat at Hannah's feet, startling the old woman every time. She swore Joseph had trained the animal to torment her for doubting the dog's usefulness. Margery could not help thinking to herself that Azeban seemed to laugh every time he delivered another bloody gift.

Samuell and Joseph often strolled in the orchard at evenfall, checking on the ripening apples as they smoked their clay-stemmed pipes. Both possessed solitary natures, but together they were inseparable and as one.

There was one favorite indulgence that farm families took time to enjoy in the very hottest of weather. There was a river that ran along the town that had a few swim holes. Even at mid-August, the water, flowing down from the mountains over and through rocky crevices and water-falling into natural baths and pools, would freeze toes in seconds. Samuell had swum in the swim hole closest to the town with the children his age when he was a boy. Now, however, he visited a private spot that was reachable only through a walk through his own woodlot and into the forest. The path was not accessible by horse or wagon and had to be taken on foot. Samuell had brought Margery and Agnes a few times and had thoughtfully withdrawn while they bathed in their shifts.

Samuell and Joseph began to make the trek most fine nights, leaving the women and girl reading or busying their hands. Margery noticed Hannah would stare after the two men walking out past the barns towards the dusky line of trees. Margery oft observed the departing figures as well. Not a sliver of evening light could be seen between the two companions as they walked shoulder to shoulder in easy companionship, Azeban alternately trailing and leading the men along the path.

Agnes's education required a contribution, given gladly, from each member of the household. Margery spent some time each day teaching Agnes, using the small collection of schoolbooks that she had collected in her years as a schoolteacher. Books such as Noah Webster's *Blue Back Speller* immediately proved to be too simple for the gifted child.

Margery discerned Agnes's natural curiosity. She began to bring her young pupil outside, armed with slate and soapstone pencil, to conduct experiments in the garden. One particular science experiment required Agnes to compare the growth of cucumbers when plants received different amounts of water and sunlight. The investigation was abruptly cut short by Hannah when the old woman discovered that a number of covered or unwatered cucumber vines were withered, yellowing, and producing stunted vegetables.

But it was the study of languages that inspired Agnes. She would take her daily slate of words, dictated by Margery to be mastered, and have Joseph supply the French and Abenaki translations. Margery found that Agnes thrived when she was permitted to teach herself. This was proven when Samuell, on one of his trips to Exeter, where they had the fine boy's school founded by Dr. John and Elizabeth Phillips, brought back Latin and Greek grammars for Agnes. The adults were ill-equipped to teach the ancient languages, but Agnes took up the books and studied them for hours at a time. She went on to add Latin to her growing list of English, French, and Abenaki translations in her "dictionary."

When Agnes had buried her face in Margery's dress rather than face the men at the town meeting, Margery thought that the girl might be immature for her age. Now she knew Agnes was unusually intelligent and emotionally intense, swinging like a pendulum between exuberance and melancholy. It had taken time for the girl to adjust to the new environment and residents of the farm. Agnes's ease and self-confidence had increased steadily as the days passed in cooperative work. The young girl held a fervent attachment to Joseph and Azeban, and Margery wondered what would happen when Joseph finished his stonemasonry contract and left the farm.

Hannah took responsibility for attempting to teach Agnes the skills needed for the kitchen and home. The old woman dictated her family recipes for Agnes to make her own receipt book. She patiently led an uninterested Agnes through steps in food preservation such as water glassing eggs, pickling, and butter and cheese making. More than one crock was dropped and broken. Whether these accidents were due to Agnes's crutch or carelessness was a matter of debate.

In addition to kitchen work, Hannah sat a reluctant Agnes down for improving her sewing and needlework skills. Agnes had learned her basic embroidery stiches and techniques from her mother, and her rather unremarkable sampler was one of the few possessions she had carried to the Wheeler Farm. Come fall, there would be more emphasis on textiles in the Wheeler household after the majority of the harvest and meat had been put up for the winter.

Samuell occasionally took Agnes with him as he cared for the animals. The girl was too unsteady on her crutch to muck out stalls or round up animals. She would watch Samuell at his husbandry chores and keep up a steady stream of questions on why humans could drink cow and goat milk but not sheep milk. Or why it was safe for the cows to graze on rye grass but not flax. She loved holding a newborn lamb or scratching behind a cow's ears, but the realization that the animal would eventually be culled for meat or due to illness always sat in her eyes.

The workday on Wheeler Farm was punctuated by the clatter of rocks rolled on and off the stone scow. The first order of business in wall building was to get the granite to where the wall was under construction. Joseph's ox, Mahom, a truly ancient creature, dragged the heavier stones on the stone boat. A handbarrow transported the smaller ones. Where the wall was to sit, Joseph dug a foundation. The stonemason removed soil, roots, and debris, a few inches in depth and the width of the wall, and stomped it flat and level. Stones needed to be sorted for thickness. The largest of the rocks composed the bottom layer upon which the wall sat, partially sitting below the ground. Next, in a pattern of one-over-two, so each stone overlapped the two below it, came the lower portion of the structure. Outer face stones alternated with through stones that extended all the way through the wall.

Joseph also fashioned stiles in the wall. The openings were the width of a man to fit through, but too narrow for livestock. Many of the round fieldstones available to Joseph had to be trimmed with a chisel or split using feather and wedge to create flat and — more importantly — level surfaces. All the day long, chisel clinked on stone whose shape would be subtly altered to best serve its role. The interior hearting was made up of small stones that filled the gaps between the face stones. The stonemason employed guidelines of strong string to ensure straight planes. Sheets of bedrock outcrop provided stone for capping the top of the wall. As he worked, the cows gathered and watched him from under the wolf tree in the center of the pasture, curious but unperturbed.

The stonemason did most of the work with his bare hands, insisting when asked that he needed to feel and understand the nature of the stone to find its place in the wall. Although he was spare with words, his hands spoke eloquently as he carefully chose and stacked rock with a satisfying snick as stone fit into place, each one dependent on the other and each one contributing to the strength and beauty of the whole. His fingers and hands were abused and unlovely, despite applying Hannah's calendula-and-comfrey-infused salve on them in the evenings.

Margery liked to walk along the completed sections of the wall in the early evening. She marveled at how the chaotic muddle of stones had been transformed into a sinewy granite snake in shades of grey, silver, and black, nestled within the pasture's palette of greens, golds, and browns. She often carried her sketch book and would sit among the chirring grasshoppers to capture a delicate spider web or fallen leaf on the wall. Other times she would sit at a distance and draw the wall as part of the pastoral landscape.

Agnes would often beg of Margery and Hannah to be allowed to collect the small stones for Joseph that were needed for the interior of the wall. She would sit on a sack in a fallow field, picking stones and tossing them into a basket that Joseph would collect. At the end of each day, Joseph would thank Mahom for his great labors and Agnes would come out to hand-feed an apple or two to the gentle beast and scratch his ears, which she could barely reach.

Over supper preparations, Agnes would educate Margery and Hannah on the craft and vocabulary of stonemasonry. "The Abenaki word for 'stonemason' is *Nodapskenigad*," she would randomly announce.

Hannah would shake her head and grumble, "And of what possible use is knowing such a godless language?" Hannah had come to accept and have great fondness for the man. However, she had not lost some of the offensive words used to describe the culture of the indigenous people who had been displaced from the land where Thorneboro and many other New Hampshire towns sat. Agnes was undeterred by the old woman's disapproval.

As the days passed, Joseph, while still silent unless asked a direct question, felt less and less like a stranger to them all. Agnes was drawn to him, and he was kind to her. He made her cornhusk dolls, and in the evenings, he conducted simple French and Abenaki lessons, starting with kitchen items and greetings. Joseph called Agnes, *Nidôbasis*, which he explained meant, 'My little friend.' He told her that his people would call residents of the Wheeler Farm *Awanochak,* 'the white man.' In return, Agnes tutored Joseph, helping him to improve his English.

LATE SUMMER
1805

~ *Leavitt's Farmer's Almanac,* 1805

When Jacob Kimball, the tanner, crossed the threshold of Stanton's to buy supplies, the room fell quiet. Shopmistress Stanton disappeared into the backroom, abandoning her husband to station the counter alone. Moments ago, there had been animated discussion about the upcoming wedding of the Stanton's oldest daughter. The wedding was common knowledge to those who attended Sunday Meeting. Banns had been published, and all good Christians of a certain social standing in the town were invited. The guests would follow the promenading bride and groom from the meetinghouse to the tavern to enjoy a wedding dinner.

Kimball was one of the few men in town that the tythingman did not admonish when he skipped Sunday meeting. It was obvious from the silence in the store that Fletcher would not be a welcome guest at the wedding. It could have been the odious nature of his trade or his mercurial temper, or a combination of the two. His spurning, he reflected, was his opportunity. Hunting deer was so much easier and quicker in an absent neighbor's orchard than in the distant deep woods. He completed his purchases in silence, eschewing Shopkeeper Stanton's nervous palaver.

"Won't you change your mind?" Hannah was still cajoling Margery from the seat of the wagon. Agnes sat beside her bouncing with excitement at the thought of attending her first wedding. Samuell was adjusting Demeter and Persephone's breast collars.

"I can't bring a long face to the wedding and it must surely be bad luck for the bride for a new widow to attend her nuptials." Margery replied as she stood in the dooryard. Her arms were folded tightly against her chest.

Hannah finally acquiesced and ended her harangue over Margery's refusal to attend the Stanton wedding. Margery had not shared the specific details of her disastrous trip to town and the disrespect shown to her by Mrs. Stanton and others she encountered, but Hannah had seen the impotent anger and distress in the younger woman's eyes upon her return.

The young widow declared, "I was thinking to find some chanterelles in the forest."

"I do love those yellow buttons, but I don't like you going into the woods alone." Hannah's voice rose once again.

"I've been hunting mushrooms since I could walk. You worry too much," Margery rejoined. "And besides, Joseph will be around here somewhere, should I have a need."

"As you wish," Hannah relented, "but your absence will be gossiped about."

"That is most certainly a price I can accept," Margery assured the old woman. She turned away and breathed a sigh of relief.

Jacob, like all hunters, knew that deer visited open fields and orchards most commonly at dawn and dusk. But he had to leave instructions for the day with his beetle-headed apprentices and wait until the residents of the town had ridden their wagons past the tannery into town for the nuptial ceremony and reception. It was midmorning before he had made his way to the largest and best-tended orchard in town, the Wheeler Farm.

Margery looked up from her weeding and watering of the kitchen garden and noticed that the sun had slid farther along in its arc towards midday than she had expected. "Come on sluggard," she chastised herself. She jumped to her feet and grabbed her foraging basket. She reached for her sheathed foraging knife that lay on the ground nearby and threw it in the basket, thinking to return it to its proper place, hanging from a leather cord around her neck, before she came to the edge of the woods.

She headed up the hill, cutting through the apple orchard to reach the edge of the farm's woodlot. The heady smell of pippins replaced the scents of the barnyard as she progressed. Honeybees and wasps alike flitted through the air and feasted on ripe and rotting apples. As Margery traversed the orchard, she remembered the spring morels she had found under the older apple trees and the sweet taste of the mushrooms and oniony ramps cooked in butter in the skillet earlier in the year. She looked forward to a basket brimming with chanterelles and preparing them for the members of the household. Perhaps she would even bake a beef and mushroom pie come Saturday baking day.

The overwhelming fetor of death rudely thrust away Margery's savory olfactory memory. Just one row of trees sat between Margery and the forest edge. She wondered if there was a nearby half-eaten animal carcass left from a predator's recent kill.

"Mistress Turner, this is an unexpected meeting. I feel most fortunate, I do." Margery turned in horror towards the unctuous voice of the tanner. He stood in the orchard row with legs anchored wide, wearing a hunting frock secured with a wide leather belt.

"Mr. Kimball, what are you doing here?" she stuttered.

"Oh, I was following tracks and must have not been paying attention and found myself in your master's orchard," he replied. "I would have imagined that you would be at the wedding today. Does your master leave you home to make yourself pretty for his arrival back to his bed tonight?" He ran his eyes appraisingly over her body. Again, the vile accusation.

"Such words are beneath contempt, Mr. Kimball. I insist you leave this property immediately. You do not have Samuell's permission to be here or to hunt here."

"Oh, Samuell, is it," Kimball sneered. "I do not know of many servants who call their master by his Christian name."

"I am not his servant," she retorted. "I willingly provide my hands to work to maintain this farm."

Margery's protests were met with a mocking laugh from the tanner. "I'm sure it is more than your hands you give to the master of this farm."

A seething rage bubbled in her chest. Then fear overcame that rage as the tanner took a step closer to Margery and slowly crouched to put his rifle on the ground. He stood back up and cocked his head, then said, "I think I have tracked something even better than a buck. I have found myself a big-eyed doe all alone." His thick, red-chapped fingers flexed by his side. Margery dropped her basket and turned to flee towards the farmhouse.

The bottom of the hill looked as if it sat at the far end of the world. She held her skirts and tried to run, slowing as she slid on a rotten apple. She heard him curse and pant as he pursued her. "Come here, slut." His voice was close. She could hear and feel her ragged breath tearing her throat. Kimball reached and grabbed a handful of skirts and she was jerked back and off her feet. Kneeling, he began pulling Margery towards him. She scrabbled, fingers and boots digging into the dirt but finding no purchase. She could see the filth under his fingernails and the manic glint in his eyes.

Abruptly, the tanner's eyes turned away from Margery and stared up with mouth agape. Margery turned, and Joseph was standing in the orchard lane, eyes now more obsidian than brown. Only the heaving of his chest gave evidence that he was not a statue. Azeban stood next to his master, hackles up and gums pulled back, exposing sharp canine fangs.

"Well," Kimball panted as he released Margery's skirts but remained in a crouch. Margery sprung to her feet and stepped back as the men sized up each other. "I had heard Samuell had taken in a hired man. I didn't realize he had gotten himself an Injun. Quite a household Samuell has put together for himself." Joseph remained still. "Be gone, man. This is no business of yours. Or is she rutting with you too?" Jacob spat.

Joseph turned his eyes to Margery. "Mistress Turner," he said quietly, "shall I rid the orchard of this vermin?" He turned his expressionless eyes back to Kimball.

"You filthy animal. How dare you speak of me in such a manner." The tanner scrambled to his feet, vowing, "I'll teach you respect."

Joseph took a step closer to Kimball. Joseph had no gun, but a handmade bow and quiver of arrows was strung across his back. His eyes held no fear of the apoplectic tanner. The sinewy stonemason towered over the squat, bandy-legged tanner whose face was progressively reddening with exertion and fury. Azeban began to growl deep within his noble chest, but still moved not a muscle.

Margery faced her assailant. "Jacob Kimball," she said, "I demand once again that you respect my choice that I will neither marry nor lie with another man as a widow of a good and beloved husband. Leave now and never return without invite from the master of this farm again."

"Shut up whore!" Kimball shrieked. "What do you think will happen when I tell the town that you are laying with two men up here on Samuell's precious mountain and that this Indian threatened to lay his hands on me and promised me death?" His eyes were wild with fury. "He will hang, and your disgrace will deepen even further. No one will take the word of a pauper and a filthy Indian over the word of a businessman who so faithfully serves the town. And then I'll be back for you and perhaps that little crooked girl." The tanner spat out the words and turned back to Joseph with a look of triumph.

Joseph spoke to Margery without breaking eye contact with Kimball's gloating stare. "Mistress, I await your instructions."

Margery stepped forward and snatched the bone-handled iron skinning knife tucked into Kimball's belt. Without conscious thought, she stepped around to face him and thrust the blade in and out of the bulging artery in the tanner's throat. His horrified gaze shifted from Joseph to her and widened in surprise. A spray of blood spattered onto Margery, hitting her face and frock. A drop that had hit her lips made its way into her parted mouth and she tasted the copper. Her hand, still grasping the knife, was smeared in gore as well. Kimball's eyes locked on Margery, and his mouth formed the word "you" but no word emerged. He dropped to his knees while his hands rose to try to stop the pumping blood. Within a minute he was dead.

Joseph stepped to Margery's side and tried to take the knife out of her hands, but her grip on the weapon could not be broken. He stepped around to face the benumbed woman and stooped to make eye contact and bring her to attention. "Return to the farmhouse. Wash yourself and your garments. Bury that knife in the woods," Joseph ordered Margery in a voice she had never heard before. "When you finish," he continued, "bring some buckets of water back here and throw it on this spot. Bring some feathers from the chicken coop. Scatter them in the area. I will take the body away."

Margery shook herself to reason and shoved the knife into her apron pocket. With a nod, she turned and ran a straight line through the apple trees to the farmhouse. Looking back before entering the farmhouse, she saw Joseph collecting the handcart, a shovel and axe, and some grain sacks, Azeban at his side. She went into the kitchen to retrieve a pail for water and some lye soap. When she stepped outside again, and looked towards the orchard, there was no sign of Joseph, Azeban, or Kimball's body.

On quivering legs, Margery crossed the yard to the well. She felt weak and almost unable to stand. The heavy iron of the knife clinked off a stone as she tossed her apron onto the ground. She recovered the garment, removed the knife, and laid it by the well. She finished stripping down to her shift and began her bloody ablutions. She washed the blood from her hands, arms, and face. She scrubbed her clothes in a bucket and desperately hoped for no visitors or an early return of Samuell, Hannah, and Agnes. Finally, she rinsed the blood off the knife, feeling almost removed from her body and senses as she completed the task. Her face flushed with heat and her heart raced. She waited to feel regret.

When she was finished, she hung her wet bodice, skirt, and apron over some bushes and ran back inside the farmhouse to put on a fresh gown over her linen chemise. Returning to the well, she stood with the knife in her hands. Her entire body was quivering as the surge of adrenaline began to subside. She stumbled a few steps towards the barn and breathed, trying to calm herself. She walked a few steps more, bending over to dispel the dizziness.

She placed one hand on the rough wood siding of the barn and walked along the periphery towards the rear. The wooden structure of the barn sat over a three-sided dirt cellar with walls of foundation stone. Her senses seemed to be hypersensitive, and she noticed the transition from running her hand along the sun-warmed wooden boards to the dim cool of the scaly stone in the cellar where farm equipment was stored.

This wall was unlike Joseph's fine stonemasonry. The foundation stones were larger, rougher, and unchiseled. Margery stopped to examine the wall and noticed a shelf created by a gap between two large stones at the height of her waist. She lifted her arm and shoved the knife into the crevice. She could not hold the weapon another minute.

Margery emerged back into the daylight, walked around the barn, and headed for the chicken coop to collect feathers. She returned to the well and collected a bucket of water and hauled water and feathers up the hill into the orchard. She poured the water on the blood stain, sending a thin red stream cascading down the hill. She scattered a few white feathers in the area, brushing them red on the blood-stained grass, to suggest a hawk or fox had caught a bird and enjoyed a feast. Finishing this task, she returned down the hill, thinking that she would be hard-pressed to explain why she had been carrying a water bucket up into the orchard.

Margery retrieved her still-damp clothes, entered the kitchen and sat at the table, expelling a tremulous breath. Her heartbeat seemed to move into her stomach. She looked around the room. Nothing in this interior had changed, but she was a different woman. A murderer. Her attention was drawn to the empty spider skillet in the hearth. The mushrooms. The thought pushed through the fog in her brain. She blanched, her mouth dry. *Hannah is expecting mushrooms for dinner.* With nausea rising even further up her esophagus, Margery stood. She swayed and reached out to put her hands on the table to steady herself.

She would have to go into the woods. The young widow climbed the stairs and threw her damp clothing onto the bed. Margery descended the stairs and stepped out of the farmhouse, returning to dwell in the relentless gaze of the witnessing sun.

Where did she drop her mushroom basket and foraging knife? Still in the orchard? She gazed up the hill and forced herself to begin walking. The apples trees, witnesses to her crime, watched her with condemning eyes. She found the mushroom basket and the still-sheathed knife. The basket had rolled downhill from where she and Joseph had encountered Kimball. It lay on its side, up again the trunk of an apple tree heavy with Greenings, easily identified by their bright chartreuse color. The knife was a few feet away. She picked up the basket and blade and trudged on. Light tracks from the handcart bent the grass and headed uphill.

Margery turned down the hill and crossed two apple rows and then turned right and headed towards the cool woodland in a different direction than Joseph had taken. She knew that this late in the season, the best chance for chanterelles would be deep in the shade under oak, beech, or, ideally, a virgin stand of white pine. The recent warmth and rain gave hope for a final burst of growth of the fungi before the inevitable cold weather set in. Margery thought of none of this as she walked in a daze for perhaps an eighth of a mile and stopped. She shook herself and took notice of her environment. She knew she needed to slow down, look, and more importantly, smell.

Breathing deeply, Margery tried to clear the scent of the tanner out of her nostrils. The scents of leaf mold, damp bark, and a whiff of balsam tumbled over each other. The one aroma in particular that she sought was the smell of sweetmeats, like sweet apricots. The golden chanterelles would stand out, orange beacons amidst the forest floor litter of russet oak leaves and emerald Christmas fern.

Her mother had taught her the difference between the savory golden chanterelles and their look-alikes. There were the bowel-disrupting jack-o'-lantern mushrooms that preferred to grow in dense clusters on wood. Then there were the trickier false chanterelles that did indeed resemble their true cousin in many ways. Fortunately for the hunters of the delicacies, both the jack-o'-lantern and false chanterelle smelled more of mushroom than apricot.

Margery spied a flash of orange and pushed through tree branches to discover a small grove of chanterelles spread under a towering white pine. She knelt, plucked, examined, and smelled a mushroom. Confirming its identity, she began to fill her basket. In her foraging, Margery had made sure to leave a portion unharvested to ensure future bounty. Standing and brushing her skirts and apron, she turned back towards the patches of blue sky she could see through the trees.

As she walked, Margery was assaulted by an intrusive thought. *Which am I — a nourishing, godly, good woman, or a poisonous, false-faced, wicked woman?* She concentrated on her footing in the dim light of the canopied forest, as roots and rocks threatened a twisted ankle. Her face burned despite the chill of the understory. The young woman emerged into the light, stumbled through the apple orchard, and returned to the still-empty farmhouse.

The kitchen greeted the young widow and quietly observed her to see what she would do next. Margery stoked up a fire from the dormant embers and moved the kettle to the flame. While many townspeople would not consider using mushrooms for anything other than condiments such as mushroom ketchup, Margery had often made a cream soup of chanterelles that Nathaniel had adored. Since she was not sure when Samuell, Hannah, Agnes, and Joseph would arrive back home, she decided she would simply cook some of the mushrooms in bacon fat in the cast-iron spider skillet over the open flames, to be accompanied by some skillet cornmeal biscuits.

Margery chose a handful of the plumpest mushroom specimens out of the basket and began to wipe them clean with a piece of cloth and a little salt. Her hands moved in the familiar task without needing her attention. She lay the cleaning cloth down on the sideboard for a moment to push back the hair that had fallen into her eyes.

A crimson smudge had stained the rag. Margery gasped and held up her hands. Faint lines of blood sat in the folds and cuticles surrounding her fingernails. The dark line under her nails might have been dirt from the forest floor, or more of the tanner's life fluids. She took up the offending rag and whisked the tainted batch of mushrooms into the cloth. Almost tripping in her haste, she stumbled over to the hearth and threw the bundle into the flames.

Taking the kettle with the now-boiling water, she filled a basin in the dry sink and added a glug of cider vinegar. The dense cloud of steam called her to her senses before she plunged her hands into the scalding liquid. She added some cool water from a jug next to the sink. Immersing her hands, she scrubbed, this time with the pot brush and a handful of stinging salt. Finally, Margery could no longer see any traces of blood around or under her nails, although she imagined invisible particles embedded into her skin.

Margery knew she must keep moving and keep the shock from dragging her down to where she would not easily be able to rise. Her raw and scraped hands clenched and unclenched, independent of thought. She set herself to the new task of preparing a portion of the mushrooms not needed for dinner to make ketchup. This was a common recipe made in her childhood home. Her father had loved to use it on everything and her mother made it for him each summer with her own hands. Margery poured mushrooms out of the basket and took up a kitchen knife. The memory of her fingers clutched around Jacob's hunting knife, the fury that had propelled her arm as she'd thrust the knife into the tanner's neck, assaulted her.

She dropped the knife and ran the few steps toward the open door. She fell to her knees and heaved. She had not eaten since breakfast. Neither food and drink nor her horror and guilt were expelled. She placed her cheek on the dirt of the dooryard, tears making a tiny pond in the dust. After some time in her prone position, she sat up. Slowly, as if an old crone, she stood and walked to the dooryard well and scrubbed her face and hands yet again.

Eyes aching, she walked back into the kitchen and picked up the knife. Margery stared at it and ran the flat side of the blade along the back of her hand. She felt gore rise in her throat again. But she swallowed and began chopping the mushrooms. When finished with the chopping, Margery put them in a pot, adding a couple of spoonfuls of salt and a few bay leaves. The mushrooms would sit overnight and shed their water. In the morning, she would drain them and add vinegar, onion, lemon zest, and horseradish, and boil it all with aromatic spices of clove, cayenne, and allspice. This mixture would be strained and the liquid bottled.

The ketchup would be served with meat dishes or used to make gravy. Even the leftover solids would be dried and ground to be used as seasoning. Next, she mixed up biscuits for the dutch oven before going back to the task of frying up sliced mushrooms in the spider skillet. Still in search of oblivion, she scoured the kitchen clean.

All too soon, Margery heard the sounds signaling the wedding-goers' return. Clopping hooves, creaking wagon, jingling harness, and the mares' chuffing. She walked to the doorway and observed Samuell help Hannah and Agnes out of the wagon. All faces were wreathed in happy exhaustion.

"It looks as if you enjoyed the day," Margery greeted the merrymakers.

"I danced with Samuell," Agnes giggled.

"Joseph will be jealous," Samuell teased the young girl. His eyes were glazed from an afternoon featuring more cups of rum punch than he was accustomed to drinking.

Hannah's habitual disapproving frown was nary to be seen. The old woman was attempting to make her uneven way towards the kitchen. Margery thought she might have heard a giggle from the old woman. It was obvious that Hannah had enjoyed the rum punch as well, but probably ached from the long day.

Samuell turned to Margery and asked, "Where is Joseph?"

"I cannot say," Margery responded.

Samuell's eyes dimmed a bit. "Ah, but he will miss whatever savory supper it is that I can smell," he said.

"I will put aside a plate for him," said Margery, forcing a small smile.

Samuell gave his arm to Hannah, who had paused halfway to the door, slumped with weariness.

"All that sitting around listening to those old hens clucking tires a body more than an honest day's work," said Hannah, her grumbling having returned.

None of the three merrymakers noticed Margery's taciturn manner as she served up the mushrooms and biscuits. After supper, Samuell, still heady from the generously poured drinks at the wedding, agreed to play a few rounds of Draughts with Agnes. Laughter filled the room. But the young widow noted that Samuell's eyes strayed frequently to the threshold, waiting for the sturdy wooden door to open and welcome home his absent friend. When Hannah nodded off in her chair, Margery gently woke the old woman and helped her to her bed.

All retired early, some to fall asleep weary from a day of socializing, dancing, or imbibing, and one to lay paralyzed in her bed, watching the events of the day scroll on a loop through her mind as she unconsciously rubbed at her hands. Joseph and Azeban had not yet returned.

Say what is sleep? and dreams how passing strange!
When action ceases, and ideas range
Licentious and unbounded o'er the plains,
Where Fancy's queen in giddy triumph reigns.
Hear in soft strains the dreaming lover sigh
To a kind fair, or rave in jealousy;
On pleasure now, and now on vengeance bent,
The laboring passions struggle for a vent.

Phillis Wheatley, "Sleep"
Thoughts on the WORKS of PROVIDENCE

Guilt was a stone pressing the air out of Margery's chest, rendering her unable to take a full breath as she lay prone on the rope bed. Agnes's pure sleep of the innocent accused Margery with each small snuffle and snore. She feared the arms of Morpheus and wondered who he would send to populate her dreams should she fall into a slumber. The young widow was awake when Joseph finally returned to the house and mounted the stairs, his tread stealthy on the wide plank floors.

Margery was jostled awake as Agnes stirred in the dawn's light. The corners of her eyes were raw from the tears that she must have shed whilst in her dreams. Before she came completely awake, she had seen a fleeting glimpse of Nathaniel lying under an apple tree, eyes closed. His body unburned but still.

Upon their meeting at breakfast, Joseph's and Margery's eyes had met, and he had nodded slightly. The infrequent crossings of paths for the rest of the day were met with polite nods. Someone who looked like Margery completed her chores throughout the day and night. The appearance of the mushroom ketchup occasioned the roasting of a piece of beef, rinsed clean of its salt coating, and roasted in the tin oven in the hearth. The torture of the heated kitchen in late summer was made bearable by the knowledge that there would be beef for the rest of the week, appearing in meat pies and various savory dishes.

After dinner, the women sat outside and breathed in the fresh second-cut hay-scented night air. The day ended when it became too dark for Agnes to continue reading out loud from Mr. Pope's edition of *The Odyssey by Homer* to Hannah and Margery. Samuell and Joseph were walking the line where the next section of stone wall was to be built. The women and girl rose to complete their final chores and retired. Margery's and Agnes's bed felt crowded with Odysseus's *Thin, airy shoals of visionary ghosts.*

The sheriff knocked on the door as they sat at midday dinner. He greeted Hannah, Samuell, and Margery by name and looked longingly at the brown bread, beans, pickles, and cold chicken set out.

"Sheriff Cole, come sit and let me make you a plate," Hannah offered.

"No, I've got men out in the yard as well as Jacob Kimball's lads," he replied regretfully. "His apprentices came and found me this morning worrying that their master had not come home for two nights. He went out hunting and has not returned. We're putting together a search party."

Cole tore his eyes from the laden table and turned to Samuell. "I'm looking for you and your man to join us," he said.

"Of course, Joseph and I are happy to help," Samuell replied. Margery noticed that while the corners of Samuell's mouth rose in a cooperative smile, his eyes registered his displeasure at the disrespect shown to Joseph.

Margery's own face was a mask of concern, and she wondered if signs of the boiling blood that rushed to her face were visible to everyone else in the room. It was as if Hades were holding her face in his hands. She forced herself not to look at Joseph, who sat silent and still at his place at the table. Samuell and Joseph stood to follow the Sheriff out the door, and Samuell collecting his rifle. The women and girl followed the trio of men outside.

In the dooryard, Azeban trotted over to join Joseph, but the stonemason nudged the animal away with his boot and a whispered command to stay behind. Margery tapped the side of her thigh. The dog turned and looked at the young woman, a question in his eyes. He loped over to Margery and scooped up her hand with his head. The posse of men and boys departed.

Margery walked back inside and began to clear the table. She was unable to speak and was grateful, if somewhat surprised, that Hannah also uttered no words of concern, no words at all regarding the fate of the tanner. The day looked to remain sunny and dry. The wild blueberries Margery and Agnes had collected the previous day had been set out to dry in the dooryard. The women and child sat out under the elm for a good portion of the afternoon shelling soldier beans, which would replace the blueberries on the beleaguered drying racks. Azeban lay nearby and chewed on a few empty bean shells before finally learning his lesson after choking on one of the dry husks.

The dog's antics and Agnes's chatter broke the stretches of silence as each woman sat lost in her own thoughts. Though it was a blazing midsummer day, preparing food for winter was a subject always on a farmer's mind and a task always in hand. Agnes was eagerly looking forward to a watermelon to be cut after supper. Even the rind would be pickled afterwards, nothing to go to waste.

As evening drew near, the men had not returned. Margery milked the cows and tended the livestock. A succotash of fresh corn, beans, and salt pork accompanied by biscuits sat ready for the men's return. The sun had set when the men finally came through the door, smelling of horse and man sweat. They took their supper and cider in the yard, as the kitchen on a mid-July night was suffocating.

"It is most perplexing. Jacob Kimball has indeed disappeared," Samuell updated the women as the men tucked into their delayed meal. "We searched the tanner's house for some clue about his departure. We found his strongbox and all his belongings, except the clothes he was wearing and his rifle. His horse was in the tannery pasture. We searched the fields and the forest until it became too dark to continue." He paused before continuing, "We found no trace of the man."

Throughout Samuell's update, Joseph stroked Azeban's head and scratched his ears. The dog had settled next to the stonemason immediately upon his return. Under Joseph's attention, Azeban had finally finished staring at his human with the accusing eyes of a child abandoned. Margery lifted her eyes to glance at Joseph, whose face remained expressionless even while his eyes sparked a flicker of reassurance. The young widow looked away and expelled her first breath since the arrival of the sheriff that morning.

Joseph asked for leave for a few evenings. He told neither Samuell nor the women where he'd gone. Margery wondered if this had anything to do with Kimball. Perhaps there was no relation to their recent experience. Maybe Joseph had found a woman. But she knew in her heart this could not be so. Or perhaps on a warm summer night he might go to drink, although where he could do that she did not know. He would not be welcome in Allen's tavern, she was sure.

Not long after Joseph's week-long nightly disappearances, he stood up from the breakfast table one morning and said, "Nidôbasis, there's something outside that Azeban and I want to show you." With a puzzled sideways grin, Agnes maneuvered towards the kitchen door leading into the dooryard. She stood in the doorway as she gazed at a small handmade wooden wagon. "This may help you with your chores." Agnes stumped through the door, past Joseph, and into the yard towards the contraption. Margery, Samuell, and Hannah followed them out into the sunshine.

The ochre-painted wagon stood a few inches off the ground, sitting on four small wheels. There was a plank for sitting and a long rectangular basket that fit snugly alongside and ran along the length of the seat. "It is perfect," Agnes said. "There is even a basket for my books. Thank you, Joseph."

The stonemason protested, "That is a harvesting basket. You should be able to get down the rows for potatoes and carrots and such. Or help me collect hearting stone. You can sit in the yard for chores when the weather is mild."

Agnes smiled a mischievous smile at her friend. "For chores or reading." Joseph sighed in mock exasperation.

"This is a fine cart," Samuell said. He gifted the stonemason a rare smile. "How did you come by the wheels?"

"The town pound wall needed to be repaired. George Dennison, the pound keeper and wheelwright, hired me and we bartered wall repair for wheels. The night falls late at this time of year."

Samuell nodded. "Ah, your nightly excursions. I did wonder what took you away." A look passed between the two men.

Joseph turned back towards Agnes and continued, "I thought maybe Hannah would make you a cushion, so the seat won't be so hard."

"Oh, is that what you thought," Hannah pretended to protest.

Joseph continued, "The pull handle can be tucked away under the cart when you are sitting on it. I can add runners and a harness and shaft in the wintertime, so Azeban can pull you through the snow." At the moment, the would-be sled dog was perched in the wagon as if expecting to be pulled himself.

Margery reflected that Joseph had just spoken more words at one time than she had ever heard him string together. She wasn't sure who was receiving more joy from this gifting, Joseph or Agnes. Both were overjoyed, although one grinned with her mouth and one grinned in his heart. Margery finally spoke up, "Agnes, you truly have a chariot."

"Yes, yes, just like Artemis's golden chariot and her Ceryneian hinds!" Agnes's jubilation was contagious.

A fortnight had passed, and Margery had begun to breathe freely again. The women were washing up while Samuell and Joseph enjoyed their clay pipes and mugs of cider on stools in the dooryard in the late summer evening light. They watched in interest as Sheriff Cole once again rode down the road towards the farm. The horse was recognizable far before the rider. Cole was inordinately proud of his mount, a chestnut horse with a white blaze. The Sheriff often boasted that his steed was indistinguishable from George Washington's charger Nelson, who carried the general safely through the Revolutionary War.

Cole pulled up his horse in the dooryard and was greeted by the two Wheeler Farm men. He dismounted and strode over to shake Samuell's hand. To Joseph he gave a curt nod.

"What brings you up the hill on this fine night? Any news on Kimball?" Samuell enquired. Sheriff Cole lifted his nose in the air, dramatically sniffing the air and turning his head towards the kitchen, "Dinner's over, but I'm sure the women can fetch you a slice of apple cake and a mug of cider," Samuell said while tamped down a smirk.

"That would be most charitable, Samuell," the sheriff said, widening his eyes as if the thought had never occurred to him that there might be victuals to be had at the comfortable farmhouse. He went on, "Kimball has not returned or been found. I come to speak to the Widow Turner in regards to the matter of his disappearance." Cole turned to the older widow who had emerged from the kitchen holding a plate and the handle of a tankard in one hand while the other relied on her cane. "Ah, thank you Mistress Wheeler," Cole said "Could not the Widow Turner save you the trouble, with your infirmary? She is here to work as a pauper." The sheriff delivered the comment with a slight scowl as he reached for his refreshments.

"Margery is elbow deep in pot scrubbing," Hannah responded with a scowl of her own. "I was happy to come out and hear the news." The old woman had seen the horse and rider from the window and had already cut a slice of dried apple pie and poured a drink before the always-ravenous sheriff had dismounted.

Cole sat down on the stool previously used by Joseph and took a sizable bite and swig of cider before continuing. He was not able to hide the preening pleasure he took being the center of attention that came with his title. "Jacob Kimball has not returned home. There have been no reports of sighting him. I am verily sure he has not fled, as we discovered his document box, his money, and account books all in order at his dwelling. I am yet unsure if Kimball has fallen victim to an accident or foul play." The sheriff shared his update while spewing forth crumbs of pie crust.

"What does this have to do with Widow Turner?" Samuell queried.

"I am here to ask the widow about a visit she received from Kimball when she was yet living in the blacksmith's cottage." The officer looked towards the kitchen door. "The apprentice boys told me about a day the tanner came back in a rage, storming around and shouting to the roof as to how dare the Widow Turner reject him as a husband." He added, "The boys could hear him all the way through the walls as they worked in the tanning yard, and said he was in bad humor for a week."

Samuell and Hannah shared a look of surprise. "I thought that bad humor was his everyday temperament," Hannah opined.

"I need to ask Widow Turner about that incident and if she has had any exchanges with Kimball since then," Cole said, ignoring the old widow.

"Well, why don't you go on in, and the two of you can speak in private on the matter," Samuell said, gesturing to the farmhouse. "I can tell you I have not seen the man on this farm since Margery arrived. Have you, Hannah?"

"No, he has not stepped foot on this farm and has neither reason or an invitation to do so. If we are in need of his services, Samuell goes to the tanning yard." Hannah's tone made her feelings about Kimball quite clear. Throughout this discussion, Joseph stood listening and leaning in the doorway of the carriage shed.

"Ah, Kimball is not a popular fellow in this town, there's no doubt of that," Cole said, clearly responding to the vitriol in the matriarch's voice. "But I must do my duty and speak to the widow." Sheriff Cole rose and crossed the threshold into the kitchen. A moment later Agnes scuffed outside. Hannah hobbled towards the girl.

"Shall we pick mint for tea?" she invited. "We can steep it overnight and have it ready for tomorrow." The two slowly made their way around the front of the house towards the northside kitchen garden. Samuell and Joseph sat and stood with their own thoughts in the noisy silence of the cicadas.

Margery smelled the sour sweat that had burst from her pores upon hearing the voice of the sheriff outside. Though her body was drenched, her eyes were dry and seemingly unable to blink. She took up a linen cloth to dry her hands and cover their trembling as the officer ducked his tall frame to fit though the kitchen door. He handed her his empty plate and cider tankard, declaring, "This farm does have a way with pippins." Cole chuckled before rearranging his face into a more somber and appropriate expression, as the official visit surely required.

Margery turned away to place the cup and dish in the dry sink as Cole continued, "Mrs. Turner, I am here to ask you some questions about Jacob Kimball. There has been nary a sight of him in over two weeks, and I am seeking to know his state of mind in recent times. Kimball's boys tell a tale that he made a proposal of marriage to you and you spurned him, perhaps causing great anger in his breast?" He took an exaggerated breath. "And I do remember that he bid on you when you were put up for vendue at town meeting."

Margery turned to the Sheriff and forced herself to look him in the eyes, then said, "What the boys tell you is true. Jacob Kimball did visit me some months after my husband's death at our cottage. He offered me his hand in marriage, but I thanked him and told him that I was still in mourning and had no plans to take a new husband." She noticed her arms were wrapped tightly across her chest and made the effort to lower them to her sides. "I think he was surprised, knowing, as all the town does, of my reduced circumstances. He left and did not return to the cottage again."

"I see," Sheriff Cole mused and looked at the ceiling. "Has Fletcher come to visit you since you arrived at the Wheelers? Did he come to call on any one at this farm on the day of his disappearance?"

"No, he did not come to call." Margery felt sweat gather at the hairline at the back of her neck.

"What were you doing that day? I recall you were not at the Stanton wedding."

"I felt too aggrieved to attend a wedding so soon after my own loss of a husband. I did not want a mournful face to cause the bride any discomfort. On that day, it being a fine day, I worked in the kitchen garden, hunted for mushrooms, and in the afternoon made mushroom ketchup." She swept an arm around the room with an open-handed gesture.

"And the Injun?" The Sheriff narrowed his eyes and gazed toward the window. "What was he doing on that day?"

"Why, tending the chores in Samuell's absence. I did see him in the fields and orchard that day." Margery's reply was perhaps a bit too emphatic.

"Widow Turner, do you think Kimball could have been so distraught upon the rejection of his suit that he would leave town or harm himself?"

Margery could not help barking out a laugh. "What little I know of Master Kimball is that he has great love for himself. At my cottage, he assured me that I would regret my decision and that any other woman in such circumstances would be happy to accept his generous offer."

"That sounds like the Kimball I know," Sheriff Cole agreed. The Sheriff looked around the room. "Widow Turner, are you happy with your circumstances here at the Wheeler Farm?"

"I am indeed so very grateful for the kindness shown to me by the Wheelers and I have learned a great deal about farming," Margery assured the officer and herself.

"Well, I am very pleased to hear that. It was a terrible shame what happened to Nathaniel. He was a good man."

"And a wonderful husband," Margery added.

"Be that as it may, you will need to consider finding a new husband to keep you." Margery lowered her head and did not reply. "Well. I'll be on my way. Please send word if Kimball comes by in the future."

"I will," promised Margery. "Good evening, Sheriff."

Margery pondered her words. She had not lied to the Sheriff. Kimball had not come onto the Wheeler property to visit her or any of the farm residents. She had made mushroom ketchup. She had seen Joseph and he had been working on farm chores, albeit before the incident in the orchard. She mused why she would worry about telling the truth, when she had committed the much worse sin of killing a man. He had been a hateful and violent man, but one of God's creatures, nonetheless. She poured herself a mug of cider and drained the glass, choking but covering her cough as she knew the officer was still outside. She stood next to the window, unseen by those in the dooryard, until she heard the sound of shuffling hooves and creaking leather as the sheriff mounted his chestnut and rode away.

She straightened her skirts and stepped outside to join the others. Hannah and Agnes had rejoined the men. Margery could smell the fresh mint in the basket at Hannah's feet. Azeban loped over and butted up against her legs. Samuell looked expectantly at her, but it was up to Hannah to put voice to a query. "Margery, what did the sheriff want with you?" The old woman demanded.

"The sheriff wanted to ask me if it was true that Jacob Kimball had asked for my hand in marriage. I told him it was true and that I had turned down his kind proposal. He asked if Kimball had visited me here at the farm and I told him the man had not done so." Margery struggled to make and keep eye contact with Hannah. The old widow held the younger one in her raptor gaze.

"Well, I think you made a wise decision turning down the hand of that vile man," Hannah huffed. "Samuell, please help me inside. I can hardly walk tonight." Margery watched thoughtfully as Mother and son made their way into the welcoming farmhouse.

"Of course, Mother." Samuell helped his mother up and they made their way slowly towards the farmhouse. Joseph looked down at the half-eaten apple in his hand. "*Majigit aples*," he said softly. The bite he had taken had exposed a wormy rotten center. Margery did not need to know his language to know his meaning, and she knew he wasn't talking about the fruit. Joseph threw the apple towards the horse paddock. Agnes tugged on his shirt sleeve to ask for his help catching lightning bugs as the sky darkened.

AUTUMN
1805

The end of summer always dazed the denizens of New Hampshire with a final burst of hot days that tumbled into cool nights. Without the competition of showy spring and summer blossoms, humble asters preened and stood above the dying grasses. Margery opened her trunk to pull out her shawl, which had been nestled in her storage chest since summer's arrival a scant few months ago. Her sketch books and journals sat at the bottom of the wooden box, beckoning her to memories. Unable to resist, she opened the top book and came face to face with her own image.

It was the self-portrait she had drawn for Nathaniel when they were courting. Margery no longer had her own mirror, a gift from Nathaniel. She had sold it along with other vanities to pay her tab at Stanton's. Hannah had a hand mirror in the parlor, but Margery had never touched it. Indeed, she had avoided the object as if it were a bewitched object of which to be afeared. She looked at the sketched image and did not recognize the chaste and naive visage. This was a hopeful maiden who had just found love for the first time. This woman would not recognize the wife, widow, pauper, and murderer who stared at the blithe charcoal lines on the smoke-scented paper. She returned the sketch and book to the trunk, closed the lid tightly, and returned downstairs to the kitchen.

The crock of butter in Margery's hand dropped and shattered on the hearthstone as the door lashed open. A panting black shadow, a tangle of arms and legs, plunged into the room. Joseph stood clutching Samuell, who lay insensible in his arms. Hannah attempted to rise from her seat, where she had been cutting beets for pickling. Her hands were dyed red, as if already blood-soaked. Her right hand, pushing her up, slipped off the edge of the table, and she fell ungraciously onto the floor. "Samuell!" the old woman shrieked from where she sprawled.

"Mistress, he lives. He was struck down by a falling tree trunk in the woodlot," Joseph replied in a voice the women had not heard him use before. Margery cleared the table and Joseph laid Samuell down, as gently as if handling a precious child.

Samuell lay unconscious, with blood on the right side of his head and shoulders. His ear had been sheared almost clear off. A flapping arm signaled that there were broken bones. Hannah had recovered her feet and ran her hands over her son's torso and head, mixing the crimson of his blood with the purple-red of the beet juice. "Margery," she ordered, "fetch Dr. Caswell. He is said to be a fine bone-setter." Without a word, Margery hastened out of the kitchen.

Margery retrieved the doctor from his fields, for there was not enough work of healing and repairing for a physician to support himself in a small town. He arrived still wearing his linen work smock, and set to examining Samuell. The doctor looked around the room and commanded, "Please describe the accident."

Joseph stepped forward and said, "We were cutting firewood with the two-man saw. A snapped tree trunk was caught up in the branches of a good standing tree. The limb, it broke before we finished cutting it and the hanging tree fell upon Samuell. He has not woken or spoken since he was struck down."

Dr. Caswell declared that the farmer had broken his collarbone, his upper right arm in two places, and some ribs. This he had determined by manipulating the injured area and listening for the grating noise of fractured ends rubbing each other. The doctor lined the bones up and pushed them back in place as close to their natural state as he could. Thankfully, Samuell was still unconscious. Dr. Caswell cleaned the lacerations on Samuell's chest, arms, face, and shoulders and stitched up his mangled ear.

Throughout the chaos, no one noticed the silent Agnes. She had come to sit on a stool next to the table and held Samuell's left hand in her small one, occasionally lowering her head to give his hand a little kiss. Margery was grateful that the child was not prone to hysterics, so she could concentrate her own attention on the injured man.

"Mistress Wheeler, I need a length of clean linen to bind Samuell's bones," the physician said.

Hannah motioned Margery to the cupboard and the young widow retrieved a linen sheet. "Cut the cloth into strips," he commanded. Margery complied and brought the material to the doctor. When the doctor had first walked in the door, he had placed a number of leather straps in a pot of boiling water that Hannah had had the foresight to have ready. Now, Caswell took those softened straps and strips of linen and fashioned a brace for Samuell's broken bones. When the leather dried and shrank, it would stabilize Samuell's broken bones while they healed and knitted back together. He wrapped Samuell's chest in linen as well, though this would offer little ease for his broken ribs.

Samuell had begun to stir and moan. "I am concerned about what commotion he has had to his brain," the physician warned. "You must watch him carefully. If he vomits and is confused and unbalanced in his body and mind, and excessively requires sleep, he may only have a concussion, which we can treat with purging, bleeding, and laudanum. If he cannot hold his water or bowels, has some part of his body paralyzed, has seizures, cannot speak words, or bleeds from orifices in his head, he may have fractured his skull, and I would have to trepan him to relieve the pressure."

Dr. Caswell spoke the idea of drilling a hole into Samuell's brain with a handheld drill as if it were an everyday or uneventful occurrence. As a Revolutionary War doctor, he had doubtless seen many more gruesome injuries than what lay before him. The doctor handed Margery a bottle. "Add some drops of laudanum to some tea or broth to ease his pain and slumber," The physician said. He continued, "I believe the bones in his arm will heal, but if we see gangrene, then we must discuss amputation."

None in the room responded until Joseph spoke. "Thank you, Doctor. Will you return tomorrow to observe how Samuell fares?"

"Of course," the doctor replied as he retreated towards the door.

Without a word, Joseph gently picked up Samuell and carried him out of the kitchen, through the parlor, and up the stairs to Samuell's bedroom. Hannah stared after them, her face white and lined in fear. To direct the old woman's mind towards a useful occupation, Margery queried, "Mistress, shall we prepare some nourishing mutton broth?" Hannah turned and looked at Margery as if a stranger. Despite her obvious shock, she set her hands to preparing the broth in silence. There was no need for them to speak. Margery knew all too well the terror squeezing Hannah's heart.

Hannah insisted on bringing broth up to Samuell's bedroom on the second floor. Her ascent up the stairs was a slow and painful ordeal. Normally, the sick on a farm were kept and cared for in the kitchen, to keep them close to the stoked fire and the women as they worked. When Samuell awakened in the early evening, he insisted he wanted to stay in his bedroom, to where Joseph had carried him. He weakly argued that Margery and Joseph could carry anything he needed up to him. He spoke in a slurring, halting voice, dropping words and trains of thought. He was clearly not sound enough to leave his bed and soon fell back into an uneasy sleep. Some of these symptoms were those the doctor had described for a fractured skull. It also appeared he was unable to hear out of his right ear, which still trickled some small amount of blood.

As evening drew near a close, Joseph left Samuell's room to complete evening chores with Margery. Upon returning to the house, he took but a bit of cheese and bread for his supper and returned to Samuell's side with a bowl of warm water and a clean cloth to bathe the injured man's face. Margery urged Hannah into an early bed, with admonitions she needed to have her strength to care for her son tomorrow.

Margery and Agnes prepared for bed, and before the young widow climbed under the bed rug, she went to the door of Samuell's bedroom one last time to enquire if she could provide anything. As she approached the door she heard Joseph's voice, "*K'gezalmel. Askami n'lawogan ta n'wigwôm.*" She peered into the room and saw Joseph's hand gently stroking Samuell's head. The injured man was fast asleep. Margery turned from the unknocked-upon door and retired to the room and the lonely bed she shared with Agnes.

Margery didn't need to know the guttural language to know what Joseph's whispered words meant. They were words of love. Words that were passed between men and women. She knew in her heart that if Samuell was awake he would not push Joseph's hand or Joseph's declaration away. What she felt now was fear. She believed Samuell would recover from his injuries. But she feared for Joseph and Samuell. Although she had never heard words of affection, she had seen looks passed between the two of them when they thought they were unobserved. She knew Samuell returned Joseph's feelings. There was a frisson in the air when the two men were in the same room. She could sense it, smell it. It was what she and Nathaniel had experienced.

She felt joy that the two men, who had taken her and Agnes in and had protected them, might find some happiness in this cruel world. But they would have to keep their love a secret. She knew the church considered this an unnatural, immoral love. She didn't care that this was not the way most loved. She both celebrated their discovery and worried for their safety.

Sleep eluded Margery's grasp. She lay in the bed, deep in thought, thinking about the two men who had showed her such kindness. Memories from her time as a schoolhouse teacher returned unbidden. When she was a teacher, there had been a boy. Nicholas Wall. She had not come to know him very well, unlike some of her female students who wanted to share every dream and thought with her. Nicolas was diligent in his studies. Competent at recess games without being a bully. Private, not one to draw attention to himself.

Each Valentine's Day, Margery allowed the students to exchange homemade valentines. Every child had a little basket on his or her desk to collect their classmates' cards. Margery herself received many sweet notes, including a few professing earnest, boyhood love. In her last year of teaching, Nicholas Wall had been in 6th grade. Valentine's Day had arrived, and students enjoyed examining their cards from classmates. At the end of the day, students packed up their books and lunch pails and put on their jackets. The children exited the schoolhouse in single file, the girls preceding the boys. As each student passed by the teacher and out of the building they made their manners and intoned, "Thank you, Miss Farnsworth."

In the schoolyard, Gyles Chadwick pulled a decorated card out of his pocket. He called, "Hey fellas, take a look at this. I have a secret valentine. Someone slipped it into my coat when it was on the peg." Boys and girls gathered round and listened as Gyles read, "I do love nothing in the world so well as you. Is not that strange? From a Secret Admirer." He looked around at his classmates, "Aye, who wrote this? Fess up." The girls tittered in a pack. The boys looked over the girls, trying to detect red cheeks that would give away the secret admirer. Nicholas stood on the edge of the cluster of boys, not joining in their debates on which girl could be so bold. He stared miserably at the ground.

Margery recognized the line from *Much Ado About Nothing*. She had loaned her precious copy of *Shakespeare's Plays and Poems* to Nicholas, and there could be no doubt in her mind who had authored this secret valentine. "Aye now, who snuck this into my pocket?" Gyles repeated. "'Who do love nothing in the world so well as me?'" the boy mocked in a sing-song voice, fluttering his eyelashes. Before the children could notice how Nicholas's behavior differed from the rest, Margery came into the yard and scattered the flock, bidding them to go home and stop their foolishness. Her eyes caught Nicholas's now fearful face, and she pointed her chin in the direction of the road that led to his farm.

She wondered now, as she had many times since, what had happened to that boy, now a man. Although there was no longer a death penalty for what was called "sodomy" or the older British term, "buggery," it was still considered a detestable offense. A conviction for the offense could lead to loss of liberty, livelihood, land, and of course one's reputation. Margery lay awake long into the night and knew Joseph never left Samuell's side.

Before the sun rose, Margery was awakened by creaking and groaning of stair boards outside her door. Hannah was making her loud and painful way up the stairs to Samuell's room. Margery flung herself from the bed and rushed to Hannah's assistance, speaking loudly in case somehow Joseph had not heard Hannah's approach. As the two women entered Samuell's bedroom, Joseph was stirring the coals and adding wood for a fresh fire in the small bedroom hearth. "Joseph," said Hannah, "I thank you for watching over Samuell in the night. How fares he? Did he sleep?"

Joseph took the old woman's arm and led her to the chair next to Samuell's bed. "Mistress, he slept fitfully and refused to take the laudanum the doctor left. I will gather white willow bark for tea and bring it to you after I tend to the animals." Joseph continued, "He is still confused in his mind and cannot hear from his right ear. But he has no great fever."

"Thank you, Joseph," Hannah said with sincerity. He nodded in response. The old woman sat and examined her son as if examining a babe newly delivered.

"Margery," she directed, "please put some of the porridge Agnes set on the coals last night in the pap warmer and bring it up here with water, the kettle, and trivet."

"Yes Mistress." Margery departed to her tasks.

Agnes, by this time, was standing unobserved in the doorway looking between the three adults. Hannah noticed her and said softly, "Agnes, when you finish your morning chores, perhaps you can read to Samuell." Agnes's downcast face transformed into a visage of delight and purpose.

As Margery traveled through the orchard midmorning, picking a basket of windfalls to make fresh applesauce for Samuell, she walked up and into the woodlot at the edge of the orchard. She walked a short distance into the woods and saw the scene of the accident, just as Joseph had described it. A heavy tree trunk with a splintered end lay a few feet away from a disturbed spot under a standing tree with a half-sawn, half-split limb. Splotches of dried blood and splinters of wood lay on the ground.

What caught her eye was that the fallen trunk was some few feet away from the accident. It appeared that Joseph must have lifted and thrown the immense trunk off a prone Samuell to recover and retrieve his body. This was a task that even her muscle-bound blacksmith husband Nathaniel would have been hard-pressed to accomplish. She could not imagine how Joseph had found the strength, as if a man possessed. The stonemason had then carried Samuell from the woodlot to the house. But remembering the scene she had witnessed last night, she knew how Joseph had found the Herculean strength.

Returning to the orchard, Margery saw the physician's wagon approaching the farmhouse. She sprinted back to the dwelling, leaving a trail of pippins bouncing out of her basket. When she and the doctor entered Samuell's room, the patient was awake. As the physician spoke to him, Samuell's voice was still weak, and he could not recall exactly the details of his accident.

The physician turned and spoke to the women, as well as Joseph, who had silently appeared behind them. "Samuell is still a bit confused in the mind and has a slight fever," he said. "I will bleed him. Please cover the windows to block the light, which may cause his head more pain. There appears no mortification of the wound, and the straps have dried securely. We will have to wait to see if his hearing returns to his right ear." As the doctor removed a jar from his bag, Margery observed he was a proponent of leeches rather than lancets to draw blood from a patient. With no role to play, Margery removed herself from the sickroom and continued with her chores.

As the days progressed, Samuell improved in his health, if not in his mood. His stuttering and confusion had lessened, though he was plagued by fierce headaches. Hannah was both offended and relieved to be unceremoniously dismissed by her son from his bedside. She declared, "His foul temper with me is a sign he is returning to his own self. Men in sickbed are truly a sore trial for the women around them."

Samuell demanded more substantial food than Hannah's herb-infused mutton teas, a recipe handed down and kept in her receipt book. He wanted to get out of bed but was still dizzy even upon merely sitting up. Margery knew that Joseph still spent each night at Samuell's bedside. He did not seem to mind Samuell's explosions of impotent rage followed by mumbled, penitent words.

Word of the accident had spread in time with Doctor Caswell's wagon clacking down the North Road towards the Wheeler Farm on the day of the accident. A week later, without being asked, local men and boys offered a day's picking of the orchard for the early Golden Russets, which were peaking. The men arrived with their sticks, hand-made tapered ladders, and baskets. Margery and Hannah prepared a midday dinner of crocks of potatoes and carrots, a ham, loaves of rye-injun bread, pickled beets, boiled cider pie, and of course, jugs of hard cider.

By this time, Samuell was able to stand and descend the stairs, pausing in his steps as waves of nausea and dizziness swept over him. On the day of the community harvest, he dressed with the help of Joseph and sat by the cidery, where the apples were to be unloaded into wooden bins. Samuell instructed the men to put down their hook-topped wooden shaking poles. He insisted the best cider was made from apples picked from the branches, rather than those shaken to the ground and bruised.

Samuell's father and Samuell himself had grafted a variety of trees — Golden Russett, Blue Pearmain, Ribston Pippin, Bard, Rhode Island Greening, Hubbardston Nonesuch, Northern Spy, Danvers Winter Sweet, and the famous Baldwin apple known as the "Butters." The blending of sweet and tart apples was well known to make a superior cider. After the apples were picked, they would need a week set aside for sweating, to reduce the moisture and concentrate the sugars, before they would be ready to be ground and pressed into juice. Samuell greeted each man and boy by name. His nod was his thanks, in the language of farmers.

There was one neighbor notably absent in the goodwill offered the Wheelers. James Harrow had two hired hands living on his adjacent farm. He also had Benjamin Meakin, whom he had acquired at the pauper auction. Word was that Harrow kept the sot supplied with hard cider as he worked him dawn to dusk, even on the Sabbath. At nightfall, Harrow unlocked his store of rum and sneeringly doled out a jug to Meakin. Then the miserable man was allowed to retire to his lodging in the barn. The other hired men lived in the farmhouse with Harrow and his wife. None of the three Harrow farmworkers were among the men who came to help harvest the Wheelers' apple crop.

As dusk was lowering that evening, Samuell, with the assistance of Joseph, exhaustedly climbed the stairs and collapsed into a fevered sleep. Hannah was brewing more willow bark tea when they heard a knock on the kitchen door. The two women exchanged a puzzled look, and Margery approached the door.

"Who goes there?" she demanded. A throat was heard clearing. "'Tis Benjamin Meakin, Widow Turner." Margery opened the door and there stood the man she had sat next to at the meetinghouse in March, red-rimmed eyes, clean hands and face, clothes hard-worn and torn. "Will you come in?" Margery prompted.

"I would prefer to speak to you out here, if you please," Meakin said, shuffling his feet as he stammered his response.

Margery turned to nod at Hannah and stepped out into the dooryard. "Mistress, I am sorry that I was not here today to help bring in the crop," Meakin said, crumpling a filthy wool felt hat in his hands. "Master Harrow forbid me to put my work aside."

"Please don't vex yourself," Margery interrupted. "I know, better than any, the debt owed to those who took us in. I have been blessed to find myself in a kind home, and I am sorry you have not found the same."

"It is as my weakness and my curse deserves," Meakin replied. Now the beggared man lifted his head. "But I want to offer my hands. I know cidering and cider." He quirked a rueful smile. "I am doing it now for Harrow. He feels considerable jealousy for his neighbor, your Master Wheeler. Master Harrow will not deign to even use the Wheeler farm cidery, as the other men in town do with their own pippin crops." He paused and continued, "If it please you and Master Wheeler, I will come in the evenings, and if Wheeler's man Joseph can help me, we can start the cider."

Margery felt a lump in her throat as she looked at this damaged man. To do this work was a great gift to the Wheelers, to be sure, but perhaps it was even more important to Meakin. "That is a considerable generous offer and I'm sure Samuell will be grateful and Joseph willing," she said. "I will speak to them. We will be ready."

"God willing, I will return a week hence when the pippins are ready. Thank you, Widow Turner," Meakin replied.

"Nay, I thank you, Master Meakin."

He turned and strode towards the road with shoulders straighter than when he'd arrived. Margery turned her eyes up to consider the darkening autumn sky and the mystery of the human soul.

A week later, after the apples had fully ripened and sweated, Hannah and Margery watched from the kitchen window as Joseph and Samuell walked out into the clement evening to join Benjamin Meakin. They collected Demeter, the larger of the two draft horses, from her stall. They had a few hours between early supper and nightfall on these late September nights. Hannah turned towards the hearth as she spoke to Margery, "Do you know much about orchards and pippins?" she queried.

"Not particularly," replied Margery, her focus primarily on scouring the stew kettle.

Hannah continued, "Apple trees do not breed true. Plant the seeds of a fine apple hoping for a tree that bears the same fruit, and the result, more often than not, is a tree and fruit completely different than its progenitor." Margery was listening more carefully now. "Ciderists need to graft branches from the trees with superior fruit – sweet for cooking or bittersweet and bittersharp for cider. The best cider is a combination of different kinds of apples, each contributing to the cider's complexity."

Margery was now looking at the old woman as she continued, "The fruit does not need to be beautiful, something that looks pretty in a China bowl. It must carry its perfection inside."

"Truly, I did not know such things," Margery said, pausing her scrubbing. She waited for Hannah to continue, but the old woman fell silent. They continued their chores in silence.

The cider-making process started with Demeter harnessed to a circular wooden apple grindstone, making slow laps around the wooden trough. Joseph and Benjamin shoveled apples into the trough, and as the pippins were ground, the pomace fell through the sieved bottom. Few words were exchanged. The scratted pulp would be stored in baskets to season for pressing the next day. Pressing the juice out of the pomace involved pouring layers of the browned apple mash between layers of rye straw into a straw-covered wooden frame. It took Joseph's considerable strength to crank down the screws and start the juice flowing. When finished, the men would transfer the liquid into clean casks.

The pressed juice would sit in unsealed casks for a few weeks or a month depending on the temperature, and then needed to be sealed for another three months before it would be ready to drink. At seven percent alcohol, it was of a similar strength to beer, and the acidity hindered foulness such as could be found in local water and wells. While the cider would be ready for drinking before the end of the year, applejack, a much stronger apple spirit, would not be ready until mid or late winter. It needed to be frozen, or "jacked" in the barrel. What didn't freeze was siphoned off into a new barrel and put aside to freeze again. By the third round, the potent brandy was around forty percent alcohol, and not meant for proper company.

After that first grinding and pressing of Wheeler orchard apples with Meakin, Joseph began working with two hired boys during the days to mill and press apples brought from other small orchards in town. The neighboring farmers depended on Samuell's cider mill to convert their own orchards' apples into juice using Samuell's horse-powered crusher and human-powered screw presses. Days when the winds were blowing from the west were particularly busy, as the superstitious farmers believed cider was sweetest when produced on those days. Farmers would cart the barrels of fresh juice home to let them harden in their cellars.

While some cideries charged by the barrel of juice pressed, Samuell typically bartered for items and services not available on his own farm, such as beef, cloth, and the milling of his grains. Samuell did, however, sell his cider and applejack to Allen's tavern for coin.

Meakin continued to come to the farm in the evenings to help process the Wheeler orchard apples as the different varieties ripened. Meakin was silent at first, unaccustomed to being treated with respect, but eventually warmed around the members of Wheeler Farm. Samuell provided jugs of last year's cider for Meakin while he worked to kept the man's hands steady. When Samuell offered Meakin payment in cash, the laborer at first refused. When Samuell told him to put it aside for his family, Meakin finally accepted. Neither man mentioned the sundered state of the drunk's household.

Throughout the fall, a nimbus of apple essence followed Margery throughout her day. The orchard floor was littered with the decomposing last apple drops the deer had not yet feasted on. There was the never-ending daily pile of scratted apple pomace at the cidery that had to be fed to the hogs before it started fermenting, which would result in drunk pigs. Sticky apple juice was always under Margery's fingernails from long hours stringing sliced apples for drying. Her hair was scented with applesauce that had been infused with sugar, clove, nutmeg, and cinnamon while bubbling in a caldron over the hearth. Apple pie or cake was featured at every meal.

The cellar stank with the tang of juice transforming into hard cider in barrels. The pervasive slightly-burnt smell of boiled cider that had been reduced from gallons of sweet cider into a rich and tart syrup assaulted her nose when she was in the vicinity of the kitchen shelves. Every opened jar of pickles spread a miasma of vinegar fumes. They were filled with the apple cider vinegar made the previous fall from leaving hard cider jugs open to the air until they "turned."

Barrels of apples packed in pine shavings that might last until the following May were stacked in the cellar. More apple barrels were stored in the bedrooms, covered by blankets that did not mask the smell. "Not one in fifty will rot," Hannah said, imagining she was assuring the weary young widow. But Margery's nose said otherwise. She would be happy if she never saw, or smelled, an apple again.

But sadly, that would not be the case today. It was apple butter day. While cider making was considered men's work, apple butter making was women's work. Butter was rather a misnomer for the thick caramelized spread that could keep for a year without spoiling. Women would have to wrest away a barrel or two of new cider from their husbands' stores put aside for hard cider.

In what was a hot and sticky all-day affair, the cider would be boiled all day in big kettles, the best kind being of copper. When all the cider was reduced to the consistency of molasses, chunks of peeled and cored apples were repeatedly added and boiled for another eight hours or so. The apple butter was done when it was thick enough for a spoon to stand up in it and it had attained a rich, dark brown color. When deemed ready, the butter would be ladled into crocks, covered with paper, and stored in the cellar or attic. Some would be bartered for credit at Stanton's or traded for the goods or services of various tradespersons.

Hannah had sent for two extra hired girls to help with the peeling, coring, and cutting of bushels of apples and the non-stop stirring of the pots with the wooden paddles. Although polite and welcoming, Margery kept her distance from the girls, daughters of local farmers. Like covetous crows, they cast around for shiny objects – gossip that could be brought back to their nests.

Throughout the day, Hannah directed a refrain to Margery. "Keep an eye on those lazy girls so as the butter don't burn." Margery saw fear enough of the crotchety old woman in the young girls' eyes to keep them on their toes without the need for the nagging. The girls also did not want to disappoint their mothers, who were expecting the girls to bring home some crocks of the treat in payment for their day's work. Both Margery and the badgered girls were relieved to reach the end of the exhausting day, though for different reasons.

The early mid-autumn day had been uncommonly warm, and the kitchen door was propped open, welcoming the weak yet welcome midafternoon sunshine. Dinner was over. The hay was in the barn, and the crops were out of the field. Yet work was never finished. Samuell was chopping wood into lengths for the woodpile, and Joseph was in the pasture continuing his work on the stone wall. Margery noticed a pause in the clunk of axe on wood and looked out the window. Samuell stood looking at the sky with lines of pain etched into his face. They had all tried to tell him to let Joseph wield the axe. Joseph had very much wanted to take over this chore. But Samuell was stubborn and insisted he had healed enough for the task.

Margery returned to her task of scrubbing cooking pots, using a broomstraw pot scrubber as well as a cloth dipped in vinegar and ashes. Hannah was at the table slicing yet more apples for stringing and drying. Agnes was out in her chariot under the oak trees collecting acorns for the pigs, though taking generous reading breaks.

"I think you have been long enough with us to know that Samuell will never ask for your hand in marriage," Hannah said to Margery's back.

Margery was taken aback at the unexpected words and paused before replying in a voice strident in defense, "I never expected or desired such an offer." She kept her eyes on the pot she was scouring.

"Now don't get chuffy," Hannah said. "You know I cannot be but straight with my words. I meant no offense." She paused, "Perhaps you may now know that Samuell is uncommon in his friendships and in his choice not to pursue a wife."

Margery remained silent, unable to compose a response. Hannah continued, "I knew he was different since he was a child and I have lived the years afeared for his safety, should the town accuse him. I think it was the reason his brother left home, knowing he could not change Samuell with the words and commands of his God. Simon did not want to be here should his brother be found out."

Margery finally said, "I do not judge Samuell for whom he chooses to befriend. I am happy he has found some small happiness with Joseph."

"As am I, my dear. I thank you." Hannah ended the conversation and resumed pulling string and embroidery needle through the delicate fruit segments.

Even a man deeply skilled in woodland tracking cannot move silently through a wooden farmhouse. Margery knew that Joseph would travel from his cold bedroom across the attic storeroom under the roof to Samuell's room each night. A slight settling of the bed confirmed his arrival. The night was quiet until a matching creak signaled his departure from the bed to return to his own room before descending for the day. Margery noted the lack of sounds of love. She remembered her own concern over lovemaking noises with Nathaniel's apprentice Aaron sleeping above their heads in the garret of the blacksmith's cottage.

Margery wondered where the men took their embraces now that it was too cold to visit their private swim hole. Perhaps the barn. The young widow had more than once noticed hay sticking out of their hair and clothing. She thought of times she and Nathaniel had strolled together through town, attended Sabbath Day Meeting or attended Fourth of July festivities. Everywhere they went, they were recipients of greetings and nods of acknowledgement. That would never happen for Joseph and Samuell. *Is this farm their prison or their safely-moated castle?*

WINTER
1805

Nightfall came early to the hills in November, forcing Hannah to light precious candles as she worked on her needlework in the keeping room after supper. Margery paused in the doorway to watch Hannah. She was perched in front of the frame that held taut the wool foundation of the bed rug. The old woman was embroidering carefully-looped running stiches that would eventually cover every inch of the base blanket. This was a new rug, just started, and the first large stylized flower in shades of carmine and mustard was emerging from a black background.

The unembroidered background fabric had the design pattern inked onto the wool, ready to be sewn over. The ink was a leaden blue rather than the typical black ink used for writing with quills. Margery had seen Hannah soak the azure paper wrappers that the expensive cone sugar came wrapped in. The ink was extracted and used for pattern making.

The wool that had been sheared from the Wheeler sheep in the late spring had been sent out to Goodwife Brown, the wool spinner in town. Hannah had tended to her own wool for most of her life, but with her advancing age and rheumatic hands, she no longer cleaned, carded, and spun the wool from her farm.

In dyeing as well, Hannah now trusted another woman in town, Goodwife Drury, the wool dyer, who used local goldenrod, lichens, sumac, walnut hulls, and various barks. The dyer purchased material for dyes that couldn't be collected locally such as indigo, madder, fustic, copperas, annatto, and other exotics. The color would need to be bonded to the fabric with mordants of metallic salts like iron, tin, and alum and even urine. Hannah worked with the dyer to secure the specific colors she sought. Like most professional dyers, Goodwife Drury took color requests, but protected her dye recipes from even her most loyal customers.

"Stop lurking like an underworld shade, as Agnes would say," Hannah chided while keeping her eyes on her frame. Margery startled and passed through the doorway, walking to stand beside Hannah. "Misery me, pull up a chair." Margery pulled over a stool and sat on the other side of the overflowing yarn basket. "I've seen you drawing out in the kitchen garden and I've seen you take your book and pencils out into the woods. But beside mending, I haven't seen you pick up a needle," Hannah said, focused on her stiches.

"I have always loved painting and drawing. As a girl, I did some small needlework and attended many quilting bees, but I have never made art with needle and yarn as you do," Margery admitted.

"Ay, it is a satisfying thing to grow an ever-blooming garden to lay under on a cold winter's night." They sat in silence as Margery watched in admiration. "Do you wish to learn?" Hannah asked, turning for the first time and looking at the younger woman. "For I do so dearly wish to share this gift before I take Charon's ferry ride."

Without a pause, Margery replied, "Yes."

"This rug will be sold so I will train you on it," Hannah said with a wink. "Then perhaps we can make one together for our Agnes. I have seen that she has no interest in such arts, and if we don't make one for her, she will have naught to carry with her to place on her bedstead when she leaves us to go out into the world someday."

Margery smiled and added, "Her books will not keep her warm."

Hannah returned her attention to her craft. "In the meantime," she said, "perhaps you might consider your sketches to decide what pattern to use for a rug for our little tanglefoot."

It was cold enough to kill hogs. A sow, fattened on acorns and apple pomace, had been killed, bled, scalded, and hung the previous day by Samuell and Joseph. In the morning, they had cut the meat into sections and brought it in to the women in the kitchen, who prepared the meat for brining or smoking. Most of the cuts were laid in kegs between layers of salt, then covered with a salt brine. A lid was added and a rock placed on the lid to ensure the meat stay immersed. Butchering and putting up a pig was an exhausting and distasteful job, but working as a team made it more tolerable, if not pleasant. The two widows also had the task of boiling down leaf fat into lard for pie crusts, a staple in every farm woman's kitchen.

Margery barely looked up from her task when Agnes put down the book she had been reading aloud to the women and announced, "I need to find Azeban. There are some nice treats for him here."

Hannah chided to the now-empty doorway, "Agnes, leave the beast outside. He'll just get under our feet." She addressed Margery, who could not escape the makeshift abattoir so easily, "I'm not wasting a good kidney or liver on that bloody dog. That sweet fool of a girl is going to kill the beast if she feeds him too much raw meat."

Some time passed before Agnes returned to the kitchen. She walked in and reported that she had not been able to find the naughty dog. Margery smiled and guessed that Azeban was staying close to his master, Joseph, who was cleaning the area where the butchering had taken place. "I searched all his hiding spots, even under the barn," Agnes complained. "I didn't find Azeban, but I did find this, so now I can help you with the meat." Agnes and Hannah raised their heads from their grisly work. Hannah looked puzzled. Margery stiffened, and her blood iced despite the heat of the kitchen.

Agnes held up an iron hunting knife with a walnut handle. "I found it under the barn. Isn't that odd?" She smiled and held out the tool for the women to see.

"I don't recognize that knife," Hannah said, frowning. Margery's heart careened around her chest. This was her nightmare come to life. She was found, she was found, she was found.

Hannah cast an eye at the younger widow, then turned back to the girl. "Agnes, that knife looks a bit weighty for your hands," she said. "Can I watch it for you while you go back out and look for Azeban again? I have a feeling if you find Joseph, you'll find the beast." Her outstretched hand, awaiting the knife, brooked no opposition. "Why don't you take Samuell and Joseph some biscuits and cider, as well. I'm sure they would be very grateful."

The petite girl looked from the knife in her hand to the old widow's open palm. She eventually said, "Yes, I'll bring a basket and jug to Samuell and Joseph." Both women sighed in relief for different reasons. Agnes brought the knife to Hannah and slowly collected the men's treats in a basket and filled a jug. She did not ask for help, though awkward on her crutches, and self-importantly declared her departure, "I'm going to take care of the men."

"Thank you, dear one," Hannah replied.

The moment Agnes was out of earshot, Hannah confronted Margery. "You rightly look as if you've seen a ghost or the devil. Do you know of this knife?" Hannah held the object aloft as Margery looked away. Silence sat between them. Not the companionable silence of daily work done alongside each other. But a silence that held its breath. A silence that widened its eyes in inquiry. A silence that loudly condemned.

"That knife..." Margery could not complete the sentence. Hannah waited. "I...he...Joseph..." she stuttered in a small voice. Hannah would send her away. Hannah would tell the sheriff. Hannah would hate Margery for the wicked sin she had committed.

"Tell me. Does this have to do with that wicked man, Jacob Kimball?" Hannah said, her voice rising. Margery raised her eyes at the vitriol in Hannah's voice. She felt a flicker of hope. Could she share her burden with this honest woman? Holding this secret had been such a solitary imprisonment.

"I killed him." The confession hung motionless in the air. She went on, "I killed him when he threatened me in the orchard last July when you were at the Stanton wedding. He said he would take me, get Joseph hung, and come after Agnes. I cut his throat and Joseph took his body away to the woods and buried him. 'Tis Kimball's own knife."

This was the first time Margery had ever seen Hannah unpossessed of words. The look of shock on her face aged her past her already considerable time on this earth. Her jaw hung open, frozen. With a sudden snapping shut of her jaw, Hannah cried, "God bless you." She dropped first the knife and then her body to the floor and began to weep in shrieking gasps that Margery feared would bring the men and Agnes running to the kitchen. The younger woman came to kneel at Hannah's side, unsure of what to do and what was happening. She knelt in silence while Hannah cried herself out and finally began wheezing in great shuddering breaths.

Hannah put a roughened hand gently on Margery's cheek and said, "You killed the devil with his own knife." Hannah grinned through her tears and squeezed Margery's hand in her own gnarled one. "I will tell you of that blackguard so you understand you need not fear to tell me your own tale." She spoke in a voice that wavered uncharacteristically. "I celebrate his death and only wish it had been my own hand that had wielded this knife." She picked the knife off the floor and allowed Margery to help her into her chair. Margery sat at her feet. The old woman looked into the past and began her tale.

"My daughter, Beatrice, was a schoolmate of Kimball. When he was a young child, I saw no sign of the darkness within him. He seemed to laugh and smile and was not so different from his little playmates. He even once gave Beatrice a puppy from a litter born at the tannery. Beatrice remembers otherwise. She said that his temper and callousness to man and beast scared her even when they were young. When he started school, he began to endure the cruelest taunts about being the son of a tanner and carrying the stench of the tannery in his clothes and hair. The boy became a brutish and disrespectful young man. An angry loner."

Hannah braced herself as the distressing memories broke over her like a tide roughened and heightened by a nor'easter out at sea.

"Kimball had always had eyes for my girl. She rebuffed him not because of his family's profession, but because she had loved William Prescott, her husband now. When Beatrice was sixteen, Kimball came upon Beatrice alone and interfered with her. She was broken. Thank God, no child came of the evil union. She told William when he asked for her hand that she was no longer a maiden, but she would not tell him of the circumstances. God bless him, he took her still as his wife, and they moved west to New York, as I told you, to start anew. She was so aggrieved that he left his family and moved away for the love of her. He is a faithful man and though I miss her every day, I am thankful to William for saving her life and giving her a home and a family."

Margery's heart broke for Hannah's daughter as she listened to the tale of evil and good. Then fury swept her to her feet and she paced around the low-ceilinged space, holding in her screams. She had no words. One man's evil reaching into and breaking families and generations. She wished she could kill him again.

Hannah's voice rose as she went on, "Samuell doesn't know about what happened. He was heartbroken when she left and knew not why they would not want to stay and expand the farm with him. He cares not about the lines of inheritance. He just wanted us to be together." Margery swore secrecy to Hannah without having to utter a word.

They were interrupted as Agnes, Samuell, and Joseph all trooped into the kitchen. "The men want more substantial victuals," Agnes announced.

Hannah slipped the knife into her skirts. They sat down to a dinner of pork and beans, pickled fiddleheads, and gingerbread and all too soon returned to their labors.

The bed rug Hannah and Margery had been crafting throughout the autumn was taking shape. The pattern featured branching and twining flower stems rising from an urn decorated in stylized acanthus leaves. As with all of Hannah's pieces, embroidery covered the entire surface of the foundation woolen blanket.

While simpler than the rug Nathaniel had commissioned for Margery, it was still a stunning textile. Margery felt a surge of pride in her newfound artistic expression. Hannah had been a patient teacher and reminded Margery that the price of her lessons was for Margery to pass on the skills she had learned from this accomplished artist to another student in the future.

November 28th. As was tradition, the Governor of New Hampshire, John Langdon, had declared this the day upon which the residents of the state would celebrate their Day of Thanksgiving and Prayer for 1805. The day varied each year but always followed the end of the harvest season. The date was announced by each town's minister during Sunday worship in the meetinghouse. In recent years, the "prayer" part of Thanksgiving Day had been shortened from all-day service to morning service, allowing time for an afternoon of feasting.

Family members would wear their new winter clothes, if they were so fortunate to have them, to the meetinghouse on that day. In addition to his usual sermon, the minister, high up in the pulpit, would read the Governor's proclamation in full, exhorting the congregation to offer up thanks to the Great Almighty for the gifts and favors bestowed and gracious guardianship over the citizens of the State of New Hampshire and the sister states of the great fledgling nation.

As the day approached, Margery's mood darkened. This was the holiday on which she and Nathaniel had been married. Now, she would be spending it with strangers. She wished she could just be alone this day, to not be required to put on a pleasant face. But she would not force her misery on the others in the household. In the past year, she had created a mask to hide her true heart. On this day, she would put on her mask.

Though there were far fewer of the native turkeys around each year due to overhunting, there were still enough so that most homesteads would be able to put one of the ungainly birds on the Thanksgiving table. Many of the men of Thorneboro attended a turkey shoot hosted at Silas Porter's farm. A live turkey was tied to a rope behind a log. Neighbors paid a few pennies to take a turn shooting at the bird's bobbing head. The winner took home the bird. The comradery and consumption of spirits sent even the losers home happy. Samuell and Joseph did not attend this event, but rather searched for a bird in Samuell's woodlot. The two men had victoriously brought one home a few days before the celebration, allowing the household to preserve their precious applewood-and-cob-smoked ham.

As it had been since humanity began designating days of memorial, rest, and thanks, the bulk of burden for preparing a table of holiday food fell to the women of the household. The menu at the Wheeler house was similar to that of its neighbors and represented the bounty of the year's harvest. The turkey had been stuffed with roasted chestnuts, minced ham, cornbread, and herbs. Margery trussed and spitted the turkey in the tin reflector oven with the open side of the oven facing the fire. Squash and apple were cooked in a spider skillet with cinnamon, butter, and sugar. A venison pie had been prepared in advance. Corn pudding and creamed onions were put out along with a pumpion custard cooked in a gourd. The apple pie included bright, tart cranberries.

Hannah made her self-styled famous syllabub, a cocktail made of whisked sugar, cider, spices, and cream, with a frothed top. Although Hannah had been worrying for a full week before the day about using her precious china and glass, all pieces made it through the dinner and wash up without incident. There was more food than the small group could ever eat in a day, and all knew the remains would grace the dinner table for the next few days.

After the meal, all but Hannah donned cloaks and went outside. Joseph had changed out the wheels on Agnes's cart for sleigh runners. The snow had arrived early in the week and had stayed. The great plans for Azeban as sled dog were dashed when the harnessed beast refused to move forward, preferring to crane his neck to see what was happening with his humans behind him. Joseph ended up pulling Agnes around the house, with Azeban running alongside, by turns barking or biting mouthfuls of snow. When it became too dark, all trooped inside, shed wet outer garments, and played Draughts and a few hands of Whist over mugs of warmed cider.

Margery had made it through the day of Thanksgiving in the home of good people. She had covered her anguish. She knew she was not the only one with an aching heart. It was Agnes's first Thanksgiving without her parents. Hannah's table was missing her daughter and grandchildren. The old widow's husband and two babes lay cold in the hillside family plot. Joseph celebrated this day with representatives of the settlers who stole his people's hunting grounds, rivers, and fields. Samuell, his body still damaged, carried the burden of providing for all who lived on this farm. Capricious fate was never far from any living being. The group moved to retire for the night, finally able to remove their masks, some to greet lost ones in their dreams and others to greet illicit warm ones in their arms.

WHEELER FARM
1806

A deceiving January thaw had teased Thorneboro for the past few days, and Samuell decided to take horse and sleigh into town for supplies. Before he left, Samuell asked Margery to walk out to the barn. Margery collected her cloak and followed, her fear of being alone with Samuell long past.

"Margery," he said, "when I go into town today, I plan on visiting Overseer Fletcher."

"Is that so?" Margery's voice was even.

"My mother and I would like to tell him that we would like you and Agnes to stay on here, with no burden on the town, for as long as you desire. You no longer need to fall upon the town for your welfare. I need to know if this your wish as well." He handed her a letter yet unsealed with wax. Her hands trembled as she held the missive. She noticed that Samuell's handwriting was fine and bold.

Mr. Jonah Fletcher
Office of the Overseer of the Poor
Thorneboro

Thorneboro January 2nd, 1806

Sir,

I greet you in this New Year and send wishes for the health and prosperity of your family. I am corresponding with you today in your office of Overseer of the Poor for the town of Thorneboro. I wish to report that both the Widow Turner and Miss Bishop have provided considerable succor to my infirm mother and have proven quite useful assisting with the varied chores of a farm, orchard, and kitchen.

As the new year begins, I will continue my care for them under my roof and at my own expense. I must state for the public record that the woman and girl more than pay for their own care through their stalwart labors. Widow Turner and Miss Bishop need not appear as paupers for auction at this year's town meeting.

Respectfully Submitted,
Samuell Wheeler
Thorneboro

Margery felt a flood of relief course through her. "Are we not a burden to you?" she asked.

"You and Agnes have been a godsend for my mother, and I am forever in your debt for saving my life and saving this farm. It would be my honor and my joy for you to remain here a free woman and member of this family, free to stay or leave as you wish," Samuell replied.

"You give me a great gift, Samuell, Margery said with feeling.

"As you have given us," he answered.

The stone had lifted off her heart. She would not have to stand in shame again as a pauper in the Thorneboro Meetinghouse in front of her neighbors. She did not know what lay ahead, but she was being given the opportunity to craft a future for herself.

"I will pay you for your services, including the time you spent here the last year, of course," Samuell added. The words pulled Margery out of her reverie.

"I can't accept your coin. You have provided for all my needs," Margery exclaimed.

"If you will not accept the wages now, I will put them aside for if and when you choose to leave this farm." Samuell declared, his words brooking no argument.

That night after supper, Samuell read aloud from the slightly outdated *New Hampshire Gazette* he had brought home from town. After he read a few articles, he put the paper down and casually announced, "Oh yes, there was some gossip of interest I heard in town today."

"Do tell," Agnes said, bouncing in her seat.

"Do you think to leave us in suspense?" Hannah said, beetling her brow. Margery and Joseph remained silent, but Margery, at least, was no less keen to hear the news.

"Well," said Samuell, drawing out the letters in a most annoying fashion, "I heard at Stanton's that Benjamin Meakin has left old Harrow's farm to travel to his wife's family in Rhode Island to present himself. 'Tis said that he has stopped drinking and means to attempt to reconcile with his wife and children." Noises of surprise and amazement danced in the air.

"But how truly wonderful," Margery breathed, her heart lightening.

"Aye it be a hard thing for a man to break the devil's hold on him when he is so addicted to drink," Hannah opined.

"I am happy he will see his Daniel, Louisa, and Rachel." Agnes voice was more than a bit wistful.

The adults turned to look at Agnes in surprise. "When he helped us in the fall, he told me of how much he misses his children," Agnes responded to the unasked question. Joseph, as usual, smoked his pipe and listened carefully. He spoke not a word, but nodded. A slight crinkling around his eyes could be seen if one looked carefully.

It was time to begin finalizing the design for Agnes's bed rug. Margery had examined her sketches over and over again, trying to decide the flora that would inspire her design. Nothing seemed just right. One evening, Margery picked up the previous year's *Leavitt's Farmer's Almanac* off the shelf. While the current year's version hung by a string on a nail for easy access, the editions of years past sat on a shelf in the keeping room. As she opened the journal, the stem of a pressed flower slipped from between the pages. A lilac. Agnes had piled the substantial *Samuel Johnson's Dictionary of the English Language* on top of the almanac to assist in the pressing, and the blossom was quite flat. Margery held the fragile dried flower up to her eyes. A hint of sweet fragrance lingered. How hopeful.

Lilacs, brought to the New World from England, had begun to become popular in New Hampshire after Governor John Wentworth planted them around his home in Little Harbor. The Wentworths, first Benning and then son John, governed New Hampshire as a Colony of Great Britain for thirty-four years before the revolution and statehood. Samuell had brought home a cutting a few years ago, gathered while on a trip to Portsmouth. The shrub thrived on the north side of the house.

Last year, Agnes, who had never seen a lilac before coming to Wheeler Farm, cut the magnificent purple blooms and placed them in a stoneware mug in the bedroom she shared with Margery, even though the strong scent wafted in from the bush underneath their open window. Lilacs were hardy and confident, surviving the punishing New England winter and pronouncing the arrival of spring. In Greek mythology, Margery recalled, they also represented love. Margery had found her inspiration for Agnes's bed rug. The spring blossoms would be here presently, and Margery could sketch them as they bloomed.

It would be autumn before Margery would be able to place her first stitch onto the framed blanket. First the sheep needed to be sheared, yarn spun and dyed, a sketch drawn and enlarged into a pattern for transfer. Hannah had begun to exhibit ever more visible signs of decline in her physical abilities, and towards the end of the rug they had just finished, she had sat in her chair and instructed Margery on completing the bed rug. Margery wasn't sure she was ready to create a rug with only her own hands, but she would have Hannah to mentor her.

Margery had found that as her skill and confidence with the handiwork increased, she began to take a simple and soothing pleasure in sitting at the bed rug frame. There was the sound of the needle pushing and pulling rough woolen thread through the coverlet. There was the touch of the thread and needle on her fingers. At the frame, her heartbeat slowed, and she could feel the joy of creation replace the sadness in her heart that she knew would never completely depart. When the candle burned down to a stub and she needed to stop for the evening, she would run her hand over the surface of the rug, its night-muted colors inviting her to return to visit them in their illuminated glory in the dawn. She would regretfully depart for bed with lanolin-scented hands.

Throughout busy days, she yearned for the time that she could again be at the frame. Margery wondered if this was how Samuell felt about his orchard, or Joseph his wall. Gratitude lived in her heart for this gift of peace. She was impatient to begin Agnes's rug. While at the repetitive tasks of the daytime, such as laundry and dough kneading, she found herself revisiting possible designs, making alterations in color or line in her mind. Not wanting to lose a thought, she might run to the keeping room if she was working nearby and grab her sketchbook to jot a note or dash off an image, or revise the pattern hanging on the wall. But in the meantime, there was the colossal work of a fecund season on a well-tended farm.

The seasons of agriculture and husbandry are demanding and unyielding. Birthing, shearing, and culling of sheep. Turning milk into butter and cheese. Putting up winter stores. Chopping and stacking mountains of wood. Plowing, planting, and harvesting food and stone from the field. Participating in town road maintenance, as was required for every man of the town. Neighbors helping neighbors with barn-raising, harvesting, and husking. Trading and bartering goods and services. Grinding, pressing, and cooking apples. Bottling and boiling cider. Building walls.

On the subject of walls, Joseph was nearing completion of the stone walls surrounding the Wheeler Farm and separating pasture and field. The fence viewer had paid a visit and proclaimed the stone fences sound. The walls, both straight and snaking as the landscape defined, were truly of great beauty as well as great function. They would rise and fall with the frost heaves the earth threw up as the seasons changed.

The work of the stonemason was a collaboration of nature and humanity. The act of piling useless rock, one upon another, yielded a satisfying, grounding, and enduring piece of art and architecture. It elevated this maligned element of the earth and forced all to admit to its grandeur and merit. Samuell and Joseph were now discussing building a larger cidery of wood and stone next year. For this, they would have to buy or barter for stone, for the farm could not yield enough of this granite crop for the additional work.

Joseph was working on a section of his wall flanking the western pasture as Margery was returning from blackberry picking one day. The back of his linen shirt was dark, and lines of sweat cut through the layer of dirt on his neck and face. Margery herself was red-faced with the heat of the day and called out, "Joseph, may I sit a moment and perhaps you might enjoy some of these berries? I paid the brambles dearly for them." She held up her scratched arms as proof.

"Of course, Mistress," Joseph said, pointing to a recently-toppled ancient beech tree. "Please take some comfort and shade." Despite Margery's repeated requests that he call her by her Christian name, Joseph invariably addressed her formally.

Margery walked through the tossed piles of glacier-scoured fieldstone and sat on the trunk. She mopped her head and chest with her handkerchief and took the opportunity to watch Joseph close up at work. He ran his bare hands over rocks as he considered their place in the un-mortared dry wall. He seemed to be listening to the stones speak to him. Margery looked at his long dark hair and the deerskin breeches that he wore when he worked on his walls.

"Joseph, may I ask a question about your walls?" Margery inquired.

"Of course, Mistress. What is it that you wish to know?"

"Well, I have always thought that the people of your tribes that lived here before the English or the French roamed according to the seasons and did not call any piece of land their own." She hesitated, then went on, "So how is it that you came to live alone among the white settlers and practice the craft of walling in land?"

Joseph broke off from his work and sat back in a crouch to look at Margery. She worried that she had offended the private and proud man. He rose, walked over, and selected a few berries from her basket. He examined them appreciatively before popping them into his mouth. Then he began to speak.

"You know that I come from a village along the Saint-François River. My father was a trader and he often brought me on trading trips to trade with other *Alnôbaiodanaal,* Indian villages, as well as French and English settlements. My father was deeply influenced by the *Patlihôzak,* the French Black Robes. Everyone in my family was baptized as Catholic and learned the Frenchmen's tongue. But my mother and I kept to the old ways in our hearts. When I became a man, my father arranged a marriage for me to a woman from another band as part of an alliance to strengthen the relationship between the two communities. There was no way for me to refuse, so I had to leave."

He paused. Margery wanted to ask a question, but knew she needed to remain silent for him to continue.

"My mother knew my spirit and that I had no desire for this or any marriage to a woman of our people. She arranged for me to remain behind on one of my father's trading trips to Montréal. After my father departed she sent me in the other direction. I travelled south into the colonies, the new United States of America, as you now call the land. She gave me her ox, Mahom, and bid me farewell, knowing she might never see me again on this side of life."

Joseph had been looking at the ground as he had been speaking, but now he picked up a stone and studied it, turning it in his long fingers. He hefted a chisel and began chipping edges off the rock as he spoke.

"I began hiring myself out as I traveled south. I have done every job there is to be done on a farm. It is true, as you say, that my people are a hunting people, but we have also farmed the Three Sisters — beans, corn, and squash —

for many generations. However, my people traditionally do not raise stone fences around animals and crops. It was only when an Englishman asked me if I could build a wall that I found I had a skill for listening to the stone. I hear the spirit in the rock and just as I thank a deer for giving his life to sustain my own, I thank the spirit of the rock for guiding me in finding its new purpose. For the Alnôbak, creating with our hands is a prayer."

Margery picked up a nearby stone and held it. It did not speak or offer up any of its secrets or aspirations to her. Meanwhile, Joseph had chosen another piece of granite to examine, his hands uneasy being idle. He looked at Margery briefly to see if she was following his story. When he saw her undivided attention, he carried on.

"I was unwelcome among my people because I would not take a wife. As an Alnôbak, I have been unwelcome here among the Awanochak even as I lift my hands in dividing up *Ndakinna*, our land, that your people have claimed. I have had to make my way among your people and learn your customs and words. I have had no home."

The stonemason drew in a breath. "Since I have arrived at Wheeler Farm, my life has changed. Perchance this is where I belong and perchance my work in stone does not have to be only walls." He stopped as suddenly as he had started.

Margery sat and waited in respectful silence, but no more words came from the once-again stoic and silent man. "Joseph," she said, "thank you for sharing the gift of your story. Although we are very different, we have both lost our homes and our people." The young widow looked at the stone in her hand. "I think you and I are like this granite. Even if we are a bit worn away by grief and abuse, we are still strong. As the rock has been removed from the field and found goodly use in this wall, so are we finding our use where we have been tossed."

"As you say, Mistress," Joseph said and rose to return to his labors. Margery stood to return to the farmhouse. Before heading down the hill, she left Joseph a pile of blackberries on a leaf under the tree next to his cider jug.

Margery swayed and stewed in self-pity as the wagon approached the Knowlton Farm. While Margery could get away with sitting out a wedding, a husking bee was a combination of harvest and neighbor mutual aid that was just as much an obligation as a social event. Her pleas to stay home were countered by Hannah's insistence that the invitation could not be declined. When Margery argued that Joseph was spending the day on his wall, Hannah said in a lower voice, "I think you know that Joseph is neither expected nor welcome to attend."

"He is most fortunate then," Margery countered.

"Is he now?" Hannah challenged the younger woman.

The husking frolic at the Knowltons was within the one mile circle that invisibly comprised "the neighborhood" for the otherwise solitary farms dotting the hillside. Farmer Knowlton had piled up the dried stalks still bearing their dried ears of corn and sent his oldest son Beckett out on horseback to invite his neighbors to join in the husking, followed by a supper and dancing. Unlike the apple spirits found at Wheeler Farm, beer and rum would be served at the Knowltons, enough to loosen tongues for gossip and singing during the tedious task of shucking.

Demeter and Persephone joined their equine companions, pegged out in a field. Hannah, Margery, Agnes, and Samuell split up by their respective genders and ages as they approached the already-raucous gathering. Margery carried apple cakes to add to the supper table. Heads turned towards them and then back to their companions. Like bees in a hive, the neighbors passed messages along as they worked and stood ready to attack any threat to their group.

Margery sat with the women her age, most married and watching their older children with half an eye. Some nursed infants. The young widow found the conversation by turns insipid and insulting. Margery listened with half an ear to the debate over who should be able to purchase the church pew now vacant due to the death of Old Barnard. Comments were made on the quality of the calico just arrived at Stanton's. The women worried on there being no tanner and therefore a lack of leather to make shoes before the winter. This last discussion captured Margery's full attention. She wondered if the women noticed the flush in her face, her quaking hands, and her guilty eyes as she shucked.

Her terror turned to simmering fury as quickly as the women switched their attention to Margery's new life. "What is Master Wheeler like?" "Has Master Wheeler been kind?" One woman even asked, "Where do you sleep?" They were ceaseless in their interrogations, aimed at determining whether Margery and Samuell were living intimately. She wondered if Samuell was the recipient of similar questions from the men.

It took the whole of the afternoon to complete the shucking. All groaned in relief, and rubbed hands reddened from pulling the harsh, dried husks. The young men, ever looking to make anything a competition, had wagered on who could husk a basket of corn the fastest. Of even more interest was the search for an elusive red ear of corn. The bearer could then redeem it for a kiss from one of the young women. To the great disappointment of many, no red ear presented itself this year.

After a well-earned bounteous supper, it was time for the dance. This was a rare opportunity for young men and women to spend time together before the looming winter snowed in the rural households. Older members, uninterested in dragging tired bones around a dance floor, would sit and pass the time reminiscing.

Children raced around playing Tug of War, Weaver's Relay, and Hide and Seek. Agnes, with her clubfoot, had to sit out the games that required running. But she seemed to be enjoying herself sitting under a tree and watching the other children. Margery also knew Agnes had tucked a small volume of poems into her skirt in the morning as they had prepared to depart. The girl was never without a book.

The volume of the conversation had risen in direct relation to the amount of spirits consumed. The boldness of some of the unmarried revelers also increased. Not once but thrice in the span of a half hour, Samuell was invited onto the dance floor by a fresh-faced maid, sometimes pushed forward by her mother. Samuell, a prosperous single farmer and oldest son, was a valuable commodity. He had managed to fend off the potential dance partners politely enough.

Martha Stanton, however, was undeterred by her neighbors' lack of success. Training her sights, she aimed herself and her daughter at Samuell with a look that announced she would accept no defeat. She had been pleased with the marriage of her oldest this past summer. However, the shopmistress had spared herself no rest before returning to strategizing to get her other daughter into a marriage that would elevate the family's social standing. Mrs. Stanton had been listening intently as the matrons had asked Margery quite personal questions while wearing a facade of concern.

Now the shopmistress approached the bachelor farmer. "Master Wheeler," Margery overheard. "I don't think you have seen my Ruth recently. She has grown into a fine-looking young woman, don't you think?" Ruth shuffled her feet awkwardly. "She has a fine voice and plays the piano forte like an angel."

"I did greet Miss Stanton at your elder daughter's wedding, if I recall," Samuell replied. "It seems like just the other day, she was a child who could not see over the pew in the meetinghouse," he continued lamely.

"She is a beautiful dancer as well. Won't you take a dance with her?" Martha Stanton pressed and actually took Samuell's hand firmly, intending to pass it into Ruth's hand. The girl looked up with gentle bovine eyes, seemingly not having inherited her mother's ruthless streak.

"I don't dance," Samuell protested.

"Nonsense," Martha Stanton said as she held fast to Samuell's arm as he tried to step backwards away from the pair.

Margery acted before she thought. She approached the trio. "Samuell," she said, "your mother is greatly tired out. Perhaps it is time to take her home." She put her hand on Samuell's shoulder and smiled at the dumbfounded farmer.

He nodded at her before turning back to the Stantons. "Please forgive me," he said, "as we must return home." He extricated his hand from Mistress Stanton's grasp. The shopmistress, for once silenced, stared daggers at the Widow Turner.

Margery's hand burned. It was the first time she had ever touched Samuell, and she felt the heat of his body through his shirt. Samuell turned and smiled woodenly at Margery, and the two walked out of the barn feeling every neighbor's eyes upon their retreating figures. They walked over to collect Hannah from where she sat at the supper table, chatting and sipping rum out of a teacup. As he assisted his mother in rising, Samuell looked over his mother's head towards Margery. He smiled his thanks as mirth crinkled the corners of his eyes.

"You were quite helpless in the face of Mrs. Stanton's marital aspirations for her daughter," Margery said.

"Even General Washington could not stand up to that woman's onslaught. Thank goodness Mistress Stanton wasn't leading the British troops," Samuel replied as he retrieved his mother's cane.

The old woman's eyes enquired, but she knew she would hear all on the wagon ride home. They collected Agnes from the gang of children, and the group made their way home, wagon lantern lighting the way.

The mother and daughter draft horses plodded along the dimly-lit road. The adults up front had thought Agnes asleep in the back when they heard her reedy voice rise from the wagon bed.

"Why does Joseph never come with us when we visit with neighbors?" the young girl asked.

No adult responded for a few moments. Hannah was the one who finally replied, "Do you remember how I scowled when Joseph first stepped foot in our home? Do you remember I called him an Injun with distrust in my voice and heart? This was before I knew him to be a fine man." Margery and Samuell sat motionless, witnessing the old woman's confession.

"We moved onto his people's lands. We have warred, and as is the nature of man, both sides have fought. My parents taught me to fear and hate and never trust the original people of this land, and that is what was in my mind when Joseph first came to our farm." Hannah paused to gather her thoughts and continued, "I am not proud to say that it took me a while to see the man. The same goes for our neighbors. They might not be ready to truly see him. Joseph might not be ready to trust them, either. It is his choice to decide if and when to fight that battle. He decided today was not the day and that is his choice."

A sigh emerged from the wagon bed. "Humans are a hard species to understand."

"Indeed," intoned Samuell.

Mayhaps this will be her last year. The old woman had nodded off in her writing chair by the kitchen fire. Margery was preparing mince for a Christmas Day pie and floating in a state of melancholia as she thought of her own long-gone parents. Falling deeper into gloom, she thought of the holidays she had spent with Nathaniel. A celebration of just two, but a time they gladly retreated from the world and spent magical hours alone together in their little cottage. Aaron returned home to his own family for the holidays, giving Margery and Nathaniel a few blessed days of complete privacy. The small tokens of love the couple exchanged were but shadows of the gifts of their hearts. She remembered the overwhelming feelings of gratefulness that she and Nathaniel had found each other. Now, it was but a dream that wakened to heartache over and over again.

Margery shook the memories away as Agnes hobbled into the room and stuck a finger into the bowl of chopped raisins, candied orange peel, and apples moistened with boiled cider and brandy. The air was redolent of cinnamon, nutmeg, and clove, to be added to the beef and suet before going into a pie crust. It would be a happy Christmas because of this child. Someone to spoil and equally to take pleasure from her delight.

Although Christmas celebrations had technically been legal since 1680 in New England, feasting, decorating with evergreens, merry-making, and gift-giving continued to face disapproval in many provincial communities. They were seen as pagan traditions and an undeserved day of rest. Unlike small New Hampshire towns like Thorneboro, larger towns like Boston did not face the same kind of proscriptions.

As a rural Congregationalist household, the Wheelers, to all appearances, did not celebrate the holiday. However, being a hill farm set them away from prying eyes. This meant that they could celebrate the birth of Christ and make some small celebrations amongst themselves, without the knowledge of their minister, who kept to the old ways.

Margery knew Joseph had crafted Agnes a small wooden bookcase with a hinged top to turn it into a traveling library, should she ever take a trip. Samuell had bought Agnes some blank journals for her various endeavors, such as the dictionary of English, French, Abenaki, and Latin that she was self-importantly authoring.

The bed rug Margery and Hannah were working on for Agnes should not have been a surprise, but Agnes had such little interest in needle arts that she'd never looked closely at the embroidery frame that Margery had spent countless hours over this past fall. The lilac heads in shades of purple had been sewn from yarn dyed in blackberry fruit, cane, and root. The blooms sat atop jade-green stems sitting in a Grecian-style two-handled vase. The loops of the yarn making up the flowers had been cut to create a piled texture. A saffron-colored, key-patterned Greek-inspired border that Margery had observed years ago in Clara's wallpaper ran around the four sides. As in all of Hannah's rugs, the background was a deep black. Not bad work for her first solo project.

Christmas 1806. The air was redolent of fire-licked red oak logs and imminent snow. Farmers never have a day off, and feasts do not prepare themselves. Christmas day began as all days on a farm begin, with milking cows, feeding livestock, bringing in wood, and stoking the hearth fire. The goose, which had evaded being enjoyed as a dinner for a fox, had met its maker in service to the Wheeler holiday table. Under Hannah's oversight, Margery had stuffed it with sage leaves and a salted onion. It was then trussed with string, dredged with flour, and hung up on a hook to spin over the open flames, occasionally receiving a basting of butter.

The young widow prepared a plum pudding, wrapped it in cloth, and put it in a pot to boil. The mince pie, Indian bread pudding, and pumpion pie had been baked the day before and sat on the counter. Potatoes, turnips, and parsnips were put on to boil. Samuell brought up a jug of cider, holding it aloft to collect a "Huzzah!" from the kitchen occupants. It was the highly-anticipated first drink from the barrels produced in the early fall, now fermented and ready to enjoy. Joseph walked into the kitchen with a basket, leaving the uninvited cold in the dooryard.

"What did you bring in?" Margery queried.

"Crab apples, left soft on the tree. My mother used to roast them in the coals of a fire and we ate them like candy," Joseph replied.

After dinner, the adults presented their gifts to Agnes, who shed tears of surprise and pleasure. In turn, she presented every adult, and even Azeban, with a poem she had written for each of them. They had been written out on precious sheets of paper in rather unlovely handwriting, if truth be told. Penmanship was not a strong suit for the young scholar. Hannah, Margery, and Agnes exuberantly, if ineptly, sang selections from the William Billings songbook, *The Singing Master's Assistant*. This was another treasure Samuell had brought home from a recent trip to Portsmouth. Hannah prepared cinnamon-infused chocolate in her copper chocolate pot. This was one recipe Agnes was actually eager to learn.

"Shall we read the Christ Child story?" Samuell queried the gathering. As they all nodded their assent, he walked over and lifted the family Bible from the shelf. The Wheeler Family Bible had been carried from England to the New World by Samuell's grandfather. Samuell proceeded to read the birth of the baby Jesus story as Agnes stood behind his shoulder. When he was finished, Agnes reached out and put her small hand atop Samuell's winterworn hand. "Why is there writing here?" She pointed to the edge of the front cover peeking out from the tissue-thin yellowed pages.

"Why this is our family Bible. We write down the names of those born, married, passed on, and the dates. Did your mother and father not have such a book?"

"I think so, but I can't clearly remember," Agnes said, biting her lip and looking at the floor. "My mother preferred tales from the Greek myths."

"Ah, I remember when I first met you how surprised I was when you made mention of gods and goddesses."

"Yes, she loved those stories," Agnes said, her eyes glistening in the glow of the hearth fire.

"Well, come and look here," Samuell invited. "Can you find my name?"

Agnes brought her face up close to the book and hummed as she scanned the inner cover. "I found it! Here! Why, under yours are four other names!"

"Simon and Beatrice are my living younger brother and sister, and Esther and Peter are my siblings who died when they were just babes." Samuell looked over towards his mother.

"Oh," Agnes swallowed, her own sad memories surely swimming up. The young girl paused then resumed her interrogation. "And above your name are the names of your mother and father. So, when you are married and have a baby, the names of your wife and children will go here?" The adults in the room sat awkwardly for a moment.

"Yes, wives and children have their names written in family Bibles," Samuell vaguely confirmed.

Agnes sighed and reached out as if to touch the page. "I wonder if I am in a Bible that my father took with him when he left."

Samuell looked pensive and did not respond immediately. He looked at his mother, and they spoke without words across the room. Hannah nodded and Samuell looked into Agnes's eyes. "You know," he started, "you are part of our family now, don't you?" Agnes was uncharacteristically mute.

"Indeed," he continued, "everyone in this room is part of a family who works together. Everyone completes their jobs as they are able, prays together, helps each other, laughs with each other, reads to each other." He pointed to the Wheeler Family Bible still sitting on his lap. "I think it is time we added some names into this book."

Samuell rose from his chair and placed the Bible on the scarred kitchen table. He turned and collected his ink bottle, quill knife, and quill from a shelf and strode back to the table. He used the small knife to sharpen the point of the feather, then warmed the bottle in his large hands. He looked up and asked, "Agnes, may I add your name to the Wheeler Family Bible?" Silence sat patiently.

"Yes, please," Agnes finally whispered.

Samuell took a seat at the table and uncorked the ink bottle. He dipped the quill into the ink and wiped it on the side of the bottle. Agnes watched his every move. "What is your middle name, Agnes?"

"Verity," she replied. "After my mother."

"And your birthday, do you know it?"

"August 4, 1795," she answered.

Before he put quill to paper Samuell looked seriously at Agnes. "You know, Agnes, this does not mean you have a new family. It means you have an additional family. Our hearts are big enough to love widely."

"I know," Agnes said solemnly. In the minds of those sitting around the Wheeler Family Bible was the tragic fact that Agnes had not received a single letter from her father since he had left her on the meetinghouse bench at town meeting almost two years ago. Samuell wrote, "Agnes Verity Bishop, born August 4, 1795, joined the Wheeler family, March 12, 1805."

"Margery, shall I add your name as well?" the farmer asked.

The young widow replied, "I would be honored."

"Your middle name?"

"Abigail."

"Birthday?"

"January 16, 1777."

Samuell wrote, "Margery Abigail Turner, born January 16, 1777, joined the Wheeler family, March 12, 1805."

"Joseph, what say you?" A look passed between the men. Joseph swallowed and nodded, brown eyes bright. "How shall I write your name?" Joseph walked to the sideboard and took a handful of cornmeal from a jar. He approached the table and scattered the meal on the surface and with his finger wrote, *Sozap Wzôkhilain.* "Sozap?" Samuell asked.

"It is the Alnôbak word for Joseph," was the man's response. With eyes locked on Samuell, Joseph took out his knife and cut a short length of leather cord from his buckskin breeches. He reached up, gathered his loose hair, and tied it into a ponytail. Margery observed the purposeful gesture and wondered at its significance. Samuell bent his head to carefully copy the name into the sacred book.

WHEELER FARM
& ANOTHER LOCALE
1807

True friendship's laws are by this rule expressed,
Welcome the coming, speed the parting guest.
Line 83, Book XV

~ The Odyssey of Homer, Alexander Pope, trans.

Hannah slipped away on a warm late April day.

The bleating of newborn lambs calling for their mothers and the scent of green, living things bursting from the earth were drifting through the open kitchen door. Despite the warmth of the day and the enticement of spring-fresh smells, Azeban had slipped into the kitchen after breakfast. He settled at Hannah's feet, and the old woman halfheartedly admonished the beast. He ignored her command to leave, and when Margery next looked at the two, Hannah's feet were tucked under the belly of the dog. She smiled at the two of them and returned to her chores.

Margery turned away from the dry sink as she heard Hannah's ink bottle clatter onto the wooden floor, ink splattering. Hannah's hand had fallen to the side of the desk of her writing chair. Margery saw the old woman's hand unfurl, releasing the ink-dipped quill into a spiral towards the ground. Hannah's head had dropped on her chest and she was still. Margery knew instantly that Hannah was gone. Azeban gazed at the young widow with sorrowful eyes, and they shared the first moment of grief.

Margery approached the old woman with that familiar feeling of heartbreak. Gazing down, she saw that Hannah had been working on a new design for a bed rug featuring two trees, instead of the traditional single-tree design. Despite being drawn with a shaking hand, one was obviously an apple tree with its pink-tinted white blooms. The other she guessed to be a brown ash. Margery and Agnes had been studying tree identification as part of the child's botany lessons, and she recognized the narrow and flexible trunk with branches featuring small, unimposing, dense clusters of claret-red flowers.

She recalled that Joseph had picked up an ash branch out of the collection she and Agnes had assembled in early spring. He told Agnes that the Abenaki people believed that the mythological *Gluskabe* had brought forth his people by shooting an arrow into a basket tree, the ash. The Abenaki came out of the bark of the tree. Margery wondered if Hannah had overheard the conversation. In Hannah's design, what was unique about the image was that while the apple and ash tree trunks stood tall and apart, underneath the surface of the ground, their root systems were intertwined.

The young widow looked away from the sketch and noticed that there was a bouquet of apple branches covered with flowers sitting in a jug on the table. The trees had blossomed early this year. Fallen petals lay on the table underneath. Margery wasn't sure who had placed them there and realized that she had been smelling the sweet perfume all morning. The air of the farm was heavy with the ephemeral scent. Margery leaned over and tucked Hannah's hands in her lap, kissed her head, and ran for Samuell in the lambing pens.

Hannah was laid to rest next to her husband Edward in the family plot at the top of the hill, to the northeast of the orchard. In addition to finishing the field and pasture walls last year, Joseph had gone on to replace the wooden fencing around the private cemetery with a fine stone wall. Samuell had commissioned a wrought iron gate to grace the entrance between the stones from the blacksmith in neighboring Farringham. A towering white pine, more than a century old, shaded the graves.

On the day they buried Hannah, violets and mayflowers bloomed in patches of sunlight, and a handful of trillium had broken through the duff of pine needles along the back wall. Margery and Agnes had planted lily of the valley near her grave, Hannah's favorite. It was a flower that bloomed in late spring, and would remind those who remained of the time Hannah had left the world to join her beloved husband. The date of Hannah's death was carved under her name, which had sat patiently next to Edward's for many years. Underneath the date, Samuell added a line from Hannah's much-loved copy of *The Iliad*,

Forever honour'd, and forever mourn'd.

The letter to Hannah's daughter, Beatrice, did not give sufficient time for her to return for Hannah's funeral. But Hannah's son, Simon, the Congregational minister with a parish in Keene, came and said words at the ceremony in the family burial ground. Simon was just two years younger than Samuell. He had no bitterness in his heart that the farm was his brother's inheritance, the tradition of the family homestead going to the oldest brother being an immemorial, if unjust practice. Simon had no interest in helping to birth a lamb or pick pippins ever again if he could help it.

The young minister was respected and loved by his congregation. Although he held great affection for his brother, after just a few days on the farm, he longed for his snug ministry house. A young lady he was currently courting awaited his return. Perhaps he missed his doting, elderly housekeeper's meals and ministrations even more. As Margery studied the serious young man, she wondered about Hannah's premise that Simon knew his brother's nature, and that the younger man feared that someday Samuell might come to love a man. Had Simon left before being forced to judge his brother, should such a thing come to pass? Margery would never know, nor did she need to know, what lay in Simon's heart.

On his final night at the farm, Simon noticed Agnes in the corner reading through swollen, red-rimmed eyes, while the adults sat after dinner with cider, tea, and apple tansey. Simon asked his brother, "Did you know that a woman of the name Catherine Fiske has opened a high school, a seminary, for young women?" The minister made the mention casually, not expecting the result he received. Agnes's head had reared up, a predator sensing prey.

"Surely, you are mistaken, there is no such thing as a high school for girls," Samuell declared.

"'Tis true," Simon replied. "It is the first boarding school and day school for girls in the whole of New Hampshire, and it is said to be only the second of this kind of girl's school in the whole of the nation."

"Remarkable," Margery commented, while training hawk-like eyes on her young pupil.

"I have visited this school, and they teach the womanly arts such as music, art, needlework, and comportment, as one would expect. However, Miss Fiske's school also teaches French, Italian, Latin, English, arithmetic, history, geography, and botany." Simon took a breath and continued, "They even teach the classics as they do with the boys at the Academy opened by Phillips in Exeter."

Agnes was now on her feet, almost forgetting her need for her crutch. "Samuell, I must see this school."

The Reverend raised his eyebrows at both Agnes's use of his brother's Christian name and her apparent lack of female reticence. "Perhaps Brother, you would be willing to host us a few days so that we might bring Agnes to call on this school? Otherwise we will never hear the end of it," Samuell proposed. "Might we impose on you further to speak to Miss Fiske about a young scholar and her talented teacher? We would need the address of the school to write to Miss Fiske to request a visit," the farmer added.

"Yes, yes, yes," Agnes said, her slender body quivering. "We must write to Miss Fiske this very moment. We will bring the letter to post at Stanton's at first light."

"There is no great need to rush," Samuell soothed. "You are as yet a bit young for such a school."

"But you always tell me I am clever beyond my years. If Miss Fiske were to meet me, perchance she would welcome me. I could sit at the back of the class. I would be very quiet." All the adult faces around the table were trying to conceal their smiles.

"Nidôbasis, would you not dearly miss me and Azeban?" Joseph gently teased.

"You and Samuell would have to come to visit me each month and bring pippins and apple cake. For the Wheeler Farm has the best pippins in the world." Agnes' eyes traveled between Joseph and Samuell as she continued to speak, "I know the two of you will miss me terribly, but you have each other. And Margery, too." The comments took Margery by surprise. *Does Agnes, too, know the love that lives between these two men?*

For a few moments the room was silent. Finally, Margery spoke up, "I don't think we need to be thinking about visits or delivering pippins quite yet. Agnes, we will write to Miss Fiske and request a visit. You must be patient." Agnes emitted a sigh of exasperation as only a young girl can make, and went to seek out paper, ink, and quill.

With dark circles sitting under her youthful eyes, Agnes begged off her morning chores to compose her letter to Miss Fiske. She had worked on drafts by candle stub, and only the guttering out of the candle had sent her to bed the previous night. Agnes sat in Hannah's writing chair, and before she put quill to ink, the girl gently ran her hand over the surface of the desk. Whether in mourning or in summons, Margery could not tell. After an hour of quill scratching on paper, more crumpled up drafts, and displeased muttering, Agnes held up the missive, ink still damp. "I think this will do. Would you read this and tell me what you think?" she asked. Margery took the sheet and sat at the kitchen table.

Headmistress Catherine Fiske
Young Ladies Seminary
Keene

Thorneboro May 1ˢᵗ, 1807

Dear Headmistress Fiske,

I have recently learned that you have begun a great quest to educate the young women of this age for preparation of a life of usefulness and service. Whilst I did first fear to offer my meager self upon the doors of your school, I was reminded of the trials of Odysseus. A favorite line from that great poem that I recall often is, "And what he greatly thought, he nobly dared."

This is how I have approached my own education in my scarce numbers of years. I have a tutor, Mistress Margery Turner, who has allowed me freedom from the trite memory exercises of childhood schooling and has provided me wings to pursue my own most sincere humanistic pursuit of scientific and liberal knowledge. I have a passion for language and have begun my own dictionary of English, French, Abenaki, and Latin.

I most fervently request to be allowed a visit to your fine institution, perchance even to apply as a student. I would be accompanied by my guardian and tutor, Mistress Margery Turner. We have opportunity of lodging at the home of Reverend Simon Wheeler.

I am your most obedient servant,
Miss Agnes Bishop

Margery read and reread the letter and turned to Agnes who had moved to stand behind her shoulder. "I am quite certain that Miss Fiske has never received a letter quite like this," she said. Agnes beamed, although Margery was not sure she was offering a compliment.

The girl snatched the letter from the young widow's hand. "I shall insist Samuell take this letter with much haste to the post at Stanton's." She sanded the wet ink, folded the letter carefully, and looked at Margery. "Do you think Samuell would mind if I used his seal?" she asked, picking up the metal stamp and stick of wax from a shelf.

"I think it is proper to ask for Samuell's permission first," Margery replied. Agnes groaned and made a show of collecting her cloak. She moved with exaggerated slowness, her limp pronounced. Margery merely smiled and Agnes finally stomped out the door to hunt down Samuell.

Two endless weeks after posting the letter to Miss Fiske, they received a response of a letter accompanied by a school catalogue. Margery was bleary-eyed with exhaustion from Agnes's nightly tossing and turning in their shared bed. The girl's mood had veered between euphoria and despair throughout the wait. When Samuell walked into the kitchen with the letter collected from Stanton's, Agnes had grabbed the letter in a very unladylike manner and read the letter in front of the hearth, her back towards the adults. The correspondence received from the headmistress was brief and business-like.

Miss Agnes Bishop
Wheeler Farm
Thorneboro

Keene May 18th, 1807

My Dear Miss Bishop,
Thank you for your recent correspondence which expressed interest in the Young Ladies Seminary. As written in the school catalogue I have enclosed, with proper training we may expect women to be qualified to think with candor — act with justice — to counsel with kindness — and direct with wisdom.

I have received an introduction and recommendation on your behalf from the Reverend Simon Wheeler. In particular, I was impressed to learn of your current independent studies in languages, and your love of Greek and Roman mythology. In response to your request to visit the school, I should be happy to receive you and your tutor to tour the school, to sit for an admission interview, and to discuss requirements and tuition.

Please confirm a day for arrival that would be convenient. I understand you have accommodations available at Minister Wheeler's Ministry House and will be accompanied by your guardian and tutor, Mrs. Margery Turner.

With Regard,
C. Fiske
Headmistress
Young Ladies Seminary
Keene

By the time she had finished reading the letter, Agnes's exuberant face had dropped into a visage of hopelessness.

"Tuition," the girl said flatly. She handed the letter to Margery who read it aloud.

"We must not worry about that right now," Margery soothed. "Perhaps there is an opportunity to help with housework in return for schooling or some such option. For now, we must read this catalogue, pick a date, write back to Miss Fiske, celebrate, and plan our trip." Margery had not spoken of her idea to any of the Wheeler Farm residents, but she had a plan that, if successful, would benefit both Agnes and herself.

The catalogue was a thing of wonder and included everything from clothing requirements of durable and dark-colored clothes made in a simple style to a notice that pupils were required to attend public worship on Sunday at the church of their denomination. Agnes, who was typically rather incautious in manner, handled the small, bound volume with a delicacy the adults had not previously observed or thought she might possess. Of greatest interest to Agnes was the list of subjects taught. Of greater concern were the fees. Child and adults alike blanched when they read the page listing school charges.

EXERCISES

The English Language including Reading, Writing, Grammar and Rhetoric — Arithmetic, Geography, History, the Elements of Natural Philosophy, Astronomy, Chemistry and Botany. — Logic — The French, Italian & Latin Languages. Music on the Organ and Piano-Forte. — Drawing and Painting.

TERMS

*For the school year, 48 weeks, including board
and tuition*
  In the English studies and writing $100
  Fuel in the winter – 5
  In addition to the above
  Per quarter in the languages – 6
  "music" – 10
  "drawing and painting" – 3
  *The use of private and social libraries containing
  3,000 vols.,*
   *$1 to $4 per annum, according to the number of Books
  used.*

*Miss Fiske will present to the Parents and Guardians a
Bill of all articles of clothing, books, stationary, fines &c.
which she delivers, or which is due from the children or
Wards.*

The day of the trip to Keene finally arrived. Samuell had written to Simon, confirming the date of the visit. Simon wrote back, agreeing to host, if not enthusiastically, then with Christian grace. Margery and Agnes had attired themselves in their best woolen finery, worn under warm capes for the cold April ride. Agnes had consented to having her hair tightly braided and fingernails trimmed. The aspiring scholar was unrecognizable as the pitiful slip of a girl who had arrived at the Wheeler Farm an abandoned waif. The snow had departed and the roads had firmed up, allowing them to take the wagon, rather than sleigh. They would have to stop to warm up at a tavern along the way.

They arrived in Keene in late afternoon and were thankful for the Minister's hospitality. Margery and Agnes retired early as Samuell and Simon sat up discussing news and politics and drinking glasses of the popular cocktail known as a Stone Fence. The drink was a heady mixture of hard cider and rum. It had become popular during the War for Independence as the drink of choice of Ethan Allen and the Green Mountain Boys across the border in Bennington, the first town in the territory now known as Vermont.

The next day, Samuell dropped Margery and Agnes off at the stately home where Miss Fiske had established her academy. Agnes quaked with nervousness and excitement. She carried her journal, where she had been crafting her dictionary. The girl had also brought an embroidered pocket she had sewn, of the style women wore tied around the waist, under their skirts. Margery surreptitiously clenched a bound folio to her chest.

A young girl answered the door and brought the two visitors to Miss Fiske's book-filled office. The tall, serious-looking woman was attired in an unostentatious and dignified navy silk pelisse with a high empire waist. She looked rather too youthful to be a headmistress.

"Welcome to our school, Mrs. Turner and Miss Bishop. Please be seated," Miss Fiske invited. The two visitors sat in wooden chairs with horsehair-stuffed upholstered seat cushions. Agnes's feet swung, not quite reaching the floor. "Agnes," Miss Fiske continued, "you sent me quite a detailed and passionate letter detailing your studies with Mrs. Turner and your own self-directed studies. I would like to spend some time this morning quizzing you on various subjects. Mrs. Turner, would you please take a seat along the wall behind you, out of Agnes's sight so as she may concentrate to the best of her abilities?"

"Of course," Margery said, then stood and removed herself to a chair near the closed door.

After an hour of academic examination, inspection of the needlework, and review of Agnes's dictionary, Miss Fiske sat back in her chair. "Thank you, Agnes. It is obvious you are a gifted and conscientious student." The Headmistress looked to the back of the room to nod at Margery. "While it is uncommon to accept students as young as you are, I have always considered ability over age in building a student body. As you may know, the students here are quite dedicated to their studies, and there is considerable talent here. But I have yet to ask you the most important question." Agnes straightened in her chair. "Why do you want to attend this school?" Miss Fiske asked simply and sat back once again.

Agnes drew in her breath and began.

"I imagine this school as the stone walls that my friend Joseph builds. Each and every stone, light or heavy, round or flat, is chosen with care and serves a purpose in supporting the strong, lovely, and useful whole."

Margery watched in wonder as Agnes sat up straight with a graceful poise not exhibited in her time on the farm.

"As I wrote in my letter and discussed this morning, I have been studying with the adults who have taken me in. I have also applied myself most diligently to learning on my own behalf. On the farm, I have read *The Iliad* under an apple tree, but I have also learned compassion for fellow man and beast through watching my guardians, who took me in with no bonds of blood. I have studied books detailing the mystery and beauty of the natural world and then made my own examinations in the field, river, and forest. I am learning how to feed and clothe myself, but honestly, I am still quite lacking in these womanly skills."

There was a moment's pause as Agnes took a breath and brushed a hand over her dictionary.

"Above all, I am fascinated with language. How we use different sounding words to convey similar sentiments and when there is a word that can only exist in one language, in one place. I plan to make the study of language my life's work."

Agnes paused and turned her head to look back at Margery. She smiled a tiny smile and returned her attention to the Headmistress.

"While I would miss the farm quite keenly, what I am yearning for now is to learn and be challenged in the company of other girls like me. I want to join your students in seeking knowledge and truth and beauty. I aspire to a life of purpose."

The room held its breath for a few moments. "Quite well said, and I think you will find when you visit with some of the girls today, that this is the place to pursue those goals," Miss Fiske said, her face still steely, but with a sensitive hitch in her voice. Margery, still sitting silently at the back of the room, felt her eyes brim with love and pride.

The headmistress sat thoughtfully in her chair for a moment before rising. "Our Head Girl, Evangeline, will give you a tour of our school and farm. You may observe some classes before joining the girls at dinner. I would like to spend some time with Mrs. Turner." Miss Fiske seemed not to notice Agnes's twisted foot and crutch as the girl rose from her seat. The headmistress stepped out to collect Evangeline from the classroom across the hall, introduced the two girls, and the young women departed.

"Your charge is very impressive, Mrs. Turner," Miss Fiske began, now settled back into her seat behind her desk. "You should be proud of your work with her education. Do you have a teaching background?"

"I was a teacher at the schoolhouse in Warrington for four years before moving to Thorneboro. Agnes, as you can imagine, is an ideal student to tutor. It has been very gratifying."

"Challenging, as well, I presume," the Headmistress pressed.

"Well, I cannot deny she is greatly excited by her studies," Margery admitted.

"And in your lap, is that more of Agnes's work?" Miss Fiske queried.

"Actually, it is some of the lessons I put together for Agnes." She handed the headmistress the portfolio. "As you can see, she requires lessons far beyond the 8th grade level. There are also examples of my own artwork. I tutor Agnes in the arts as well, but she has such an affinity for languages and ancient history, it is hard to get her to concentrate on pencil, charcoal, or watercolor." Margery added, "But it is a subject I dearly love to teach."

"And why are you showing me these?" Miss Fiske asked, a small smile playing on her lips.

Margery took a deep breath then said, "I am presenting these materials to you as I enquire if you are in need of a teacher of the arts. I know some English literature, botany, and needle arts as well. I have received training in the textile arts from Hannah Wheeler, a renowned bed rug mak-er. You may have seen her work at the Minister's house? He has one of her very fine bed rugs in the parlor room."

Miss Fiske took her time paging through the collected material before raising her head and addressing the young widow. "I understand from Reverend Wheeler that you and Agnes have been living at his brother's farm. Do you have family?"

"I am a widow who does not wish to remarry. I have no property and have lived on the Wheeler Farm for two years, first as a pauper taken in, and then as a hired hand and companion to his elderly mother. Hannah Wheeler has recently passed. It is my greatest ambition to find a place where I can use my skills as a teacher and be part of a community such as this school."

"I too have no desire to take a husband. My family is this school," Miss Fiske pronounced. "Perhaps we have a place for you here. You must know that while teachers have room and board here, there is very little in the way of wages."

"I require no wages if you would accept Agnes, who cannot pay tuition," Margery blurted.

A slight frown passed over the headmistress's face. "I will consider your proposal," Miss Fiske announced. "Now let me show you our school."

The day sped past for Margery and Agnes, and all too soon it was time for them to depart. Miss Fiske saw them off warmly and promised to consider both admission and employment, but offered no indication one way or another that would encourage the woman and girl to think their petitions had been heard favorably. At the Minister's house, the group shared one more dinner before their morning departure. The conversation was spirited over a meal highlighted by fresh Ashuelot River trout in cream, a treat for the inland Wheeler Farm inhabitants.

Agnes waxed over the classrooms stuffed with books, maps, and globes. Margery, in contrast, was silent, thinking longingly of the sun-filled art studio and gardens for plein air painting. Samuell asked his brother if he would put in a good word for Agnes, and the Minister promised to pay another call on Miss Fiske. While Simon did not seem to be a particularly fervent proponent for the advanced education of young women, he did love his brother and so acquiesced to his request.

Agnes continued her monologue on the wagon trip back to the farm the next day. When they stopped midday for lunch, Samuell whispered in Margery's ear as he handed her down from the seat, "Remember how silent she was when we first met her?" Margery offered back a bittersweet grin.

As the Wheeler Farm came into view, Agnes's chatter petered off. This was the first time the woman and girl had returned home to a farm where Hannah was not in the kitchen to greet them. Margery's eyes were drawn up the hill towards the resting place of Hannah in the family cemetery. She noticed that Agnes was furtively wiping tears away.

Azeban, however, insisted on their full attention as he hurtled towards the wagon as it entered the dooryard. He barked fervently in greeting, trying to distract the sojourners from their returning sorrow. After a light supper,

Joseph patiently listened as Agnes once again reviewed every detail of the school: the classrooms and supplies, the teachers and students, the bedrooms of the boarders, and the farm and dairy from which the school community fed themselves. The house only fell silent when Agnes fell into an exhausted sleep.

For the next month, Agnes begged the adults every day to ride to town to check the post. In planting season this was not a reasonable request, and Agnes had to wait for mail to be picked up once a week. The days teased and lengthened.

During planting season, Samuell had hired an additional farmhand. When the oldest girl from the neighboring farm came by to ask if there was work to be had, Samuell had instructed Margery to hire the girl to work in the kitchen and barn during the day and return to her family home each evening. The addition of more hands to work soothed Margery's growing feeling of guilt over her desire to pursue a life away from the farm that had been so generous to her. But then she would veer back into convincing herself that she would never be hired by Miss Fiske, to be a part of such an august institution. She decided she needed to confess to Samuell that she had applied for a position at the school, even though she was sure she and her aspirations would be rejected.

On a July evening Margery went in search of Samuell, not needing directions. In this, her third growing season on the farm, she knew where she would find him. As she made her way up to the orchard, she heard the musical trill of a grey tree frog. She didn't bother to turn her head to seek out the nocturnal creature, as its brownish-grey mottled skin would be blending with the bark of the trees to which it clung. Samuell would be out here in the last of the daylight, thinning the clusters of small fruit to remove the diseased, insect-damaged, or undersized, giving the remaining apples the opportunity to thrive.

"Samuell, may I speak with you?" Margery called through the branches. She knew he would be most comfortable in an intimate conversation if he was allowed to keep his hands and eyes on his work.

"Is there something with which you need assistance?" the orchardist said, furrowing his brows in concern.

"No, I need to tell you of a matter I discussed with Miss Fiske during our visit." Margery steadied herself before continuing. "I enquired of Miss Fiske if there was a teaching position for which I might be qualified." She paused to wait for a reaction, but Samuell had returned his eyes to the pippins. His face was unreadable. "I know that I most certainly won't be offered a place," she stuttered. "But I wanted you to know and I was troubled that you might be angry that I acted behind your back after all your great kindnesses."

Samuell was silent for a few moments then spoke, "My brother Simon wrote of your conversation with Miss Fiske after he paid Miss Fiske a visit at the school after your departure." Margery felt her face flush to be caught out. "If you were to be offered a position at the Seminary, I would be happy that you and Agnes would yet be together. You could pursue a life far more suited for you than farmwork."

Margery was taken aback, "Has my work on the farm been so very inept?"

"No, no," Samuell's voice and the color in his cheeks rose. "I misspeak. I have never been a man of words." The farmer continued, "I am indebted to you and Agnes for giving Hannah comfort in her last years and helping to manage this farm. Except for milking cows. You truly have no talent for that." They shared a laugh. "And..." he paused, keeping his eyes on the branch in front of him. "I thank you for your graciousness in living alongside myself and Joseph. There are not many in this world who would ... accept how we live our lives."

Now it was Margery's turn to have difficulty stringing together words. "I am nothing but happy that you have found each other in this oft-unkind world," the young widow said simply.

Samuell took his eyes off his work and looked into Margery's eyes, "If you are offered a position at the school, I would rejoice with you. If not, you are welcome to live here on the farm for as long as you desire or until you find another place better suited. I have been blessed to be able to tend this farm and orchard. I have been allowed to choose my life, so should you have that right."

"Thank you," Margery managed to reply, her throat tight. As she turned to walk down the hill, she felt a long dormant lightness in her chest.

Miss Agnes Bishop
Wheeler Farm
Thorneboro

Keene July 20th,1807

My Dear Miss Bishop,

In our meeting of May the 6th, I enjoyed our conversation and was much impressed with the level of schooling achieved through both the tutoring of Mrs. Turner and your own independent pursuits. In this correspondence, I would like to offer you a place as a member of in the incoming class of 1807.

In regards to tuition, Mrs. Turner has offered to donate her salary as an instructor here at the Seminary in exchange for your debt. If Mrs. Turner is unable or unwilling to accept the position, we can be in further discussion as to the remittance of tuition. Upon completion of arrangements, a list of items to be acquired and packed and instructions for arrival will be sent.

Please reply by timely post indicating your acceptance of this offer of admission. I look forward to the contributions you will make to our school and eventually to our great country.

Accept my best wishes for your improvement in application, learning, and rectitude.

C. Fiske
Headmistress
Young Ladies Seminary
Keene

Mrs. Margery Turner
Wheeler Farm
Thorneboro

Keene July 20th,1807

My Dear Mrs. Turner,

I thank you for your visit of May the 6th and for accompanying Miss Bishop for an admissions interview. She is a remarkable young woman. An additional pleasure was had in having the opportunity to make your acquaintance, and to learn of your qualifications and interest in joining the faculty at the Seminary.

With this letter, I would like to formally offer you a teaching position at the school beginning with the upcoming school year, initially teaching a selection of our fine arts courses. In compensation, I offer room and board. I am willing to accept the forfeiture of your salary to be placed towards the tuition debt for Agnes Bishop, should she accept the offer of admission sent by separate post.

Upon receipt of your acceptance of this offer of employment, instructions, and dates for your arrival and additional details will be communicated.

With Regard,
C. Fiske
Headmistress
Young Ladies Seminary
Keene

The overburdened carriage came to a stop before the dignified two-story house. The four human occupants and one canine one sat immobile for a few moments while Demeter and Persephone stood steaming in their traces. Margery was the first to speak, "Well, we have been delivered safely..." Her voice trailed off. Agnes was staring at the school, an uncharacteristic look of trepidation on her youthful face.

After a few more moments of uncomfortable silence, Joseph rose from the bed of the wagon and nimbly jumped down to the ground. He held his hand out to Margery and then Agnes, wordlessly assisting them down from the wagon seat. Both Samuell and Joseph had accompanied the woman and girl on the trip to Miss Fiske's, planning to turn around and return to the farm immediately to be back for a late evening milking and feeding of the animals.

Samuell had climbed down from the driver's seat and walked around the wagon to where the others were gathered. "We will return to bring you home when school is not in session," Samuell announced with a clearing of his throat. "The farm will miss you." He paused, looked at the ground and added, "Joseph and I will miss you."

"And Azeban," Joseph appended. Agnes burst into tears. "There, there," Joseph said. He knelt and took the girl into his sinewy arms. "This is a day of great joy, Nidôbasis." Azeban, who had also jumped down from the wagon, ran over and wriggled himself between the two. "You must be proud of yourself and continue to work hard on your studies. We expect you to write and tell us of all your accomplishments."

"I will," Agnes fervently replied.

Margery turned to Samuell, "I thank you Samuell." She could think of no additional words that didn't sound trite. She turned to Joseph, "I thank you Joseph." Though she had repeated the same words, they held a different meaning. Both men nodded and then made themselves busy unloading Margery and Agnes's trunk. Margery pictured her bedrug sitting just under the lid of the trunk, waiting to be shaken out and placed on the bed in her new home.

As Samuell and Joseph carried the luggage up the porch stairs, Miss Fiske emerged and stood waiting for the new teacher and pupil to complete their farewells. Margery took Agnes' hand and the two mounted the stairs towards their future. The men lowered the trunk and nodded a greeting to Miss Fiske. They gifted Margery, and Agnes final smiles and returned to the wagon. Samuell, now sharing the wagon seat with Joseph, clucked the horses and the wagon set off. Not a sliver of afternoon light could be seen between the two companions as Samuell turned the horses toward home.

AFTERWORD

"Pauper," as the term is used in this novel, refers to an individual to whom a public or private overseer of the poor provides aid or considers needy. In rural New England, as well as anywhere throughout human history, really, whole families or individuals could find themselves in abject poverty due to a family member's death, debt, poor crop yield, substance abuse, natural disaster, or a host of other causes.

The American colonies, and later states, originally based their social welfare or "poor relief" on the English Elizabethan Poor Laws of 1594 and 1601, which directed towns or parishes to levy taxes for the "outdoor relief" of the poor. The laws also classified the poor into the worthy (orphaned, widowed, elderly, disabled) and the unworthy (drunk, indolent). The beneficiaries of public relief needed to prove that they had no kin existing or financially available to care for them, and that they were legal residents of the town, as determined by local residency laws.

It was up to the town fathers, with an emphasis on the word "fathers," to take care of these human unfortunates with the least tax burden possible to the residents of the town. The form of charity taken in many New England towns during the time period of this novel was the institution of the pauper auction. As noted in the story, in this vendue system, bidders for paupers bid down, not up. The lowest bidder would receive a cash stipend from the town, by the week, month, or year, to take into care one or more paupers. It was understood that unless the pauper was too aged or physically infirm to work, he or she would be put to work in the fields or household. Christian charity did not preclude a profit motive, and the typical goal of the bidder was to come out ahead financially after feeding and housing costs. The opportunities for abuse are easily imaginable.

In *Pauper Auction*, the paupers who are bid off in 1805 Thorneboro are a widow, a dependent girl living with a disability, and an intemperate man, all of English descent. They passed the bar of "resident" of the town according to settlement laws of that town at that time. Our heroine, Margery, is an example of how limitations in pursuing economically-viable occupations and advanced education, inheritance laws, and participation in household economic decisions, contribute to the challenges of unmarried women to live independent lives and weather economic downturns during this time period. Margery's and Agnes's experiences and their humane treatment at the Wheeler Farm were fictional, and most likely not representative of the experiences of many town paupers.

The pauper system differs drastically from the institution of African American and Native American slavery. Paupers were not held to the household they found themselves vendued into after the annual town meeting. A pauper could be your former neighbor or classmate. Slaves, on the other hand, were considered non-human commodities bought for life, their very humanity denied. New Hampshire abolished African-American slavery in 1783. However, cases of slave ownership in the state existed until around 1853. First Nation tribes experienced slavery as war captives, particularly after King Phillip's War (1675-1678). They could also be sentenced to involuntary indentured servitude for breaking English laws in the colonies and later, states.

Margery's husband Nathaniel had yet another experience with servitude and bondage. He arrived in New Hampshire from England as an indentured servant with a seven-year contract. While he doubtlessly had little personal freedom during that period, his apprenticeship as a blacksmith with his uncle allowed him to begin earning a living as a free man in a trade after his contract expired.

All characters in the book are fictional with the exception of Benning and John Wentworth, Ethan Allen, and Catherine Fiske. Miss Fiske was indeed the founder and head of the Seminary for Young Ladies in Keene, New Hampshire. Margery and Agnes join the school, respectively as faculty and student, in 1807. Miss Fiske actually opened her school in 1814. The boarding and day school was the first school of this type in New Hampshire and the second in the country. It operated for 31 years and served over 2,500 girls (and eventually some boys). The curriculum included science courses such as astronomy, chemistry, geography, and botany, and language courses, including French, Italian, and Latin. Other humanities courses were philosophy and history. Arts encompassed music, drawing, painting, and needlework. The school also ran a farm and dairy.

In *Pauper Auction*, the towns of Thorneboro, Warrington, Cantwell, and Farringham are fictional. Portsmouth, Concord, Keene, and Exeter are New Hampshire cities and town.

ACKNOWLEDGEMENTS & REFERENCES

New England is blessed with a bounty of historical societies, museums, and historic homes and sites. I received generous assistance from historians, curators, museum guides, and librarians on the topics related to New England and New Hampshire history found in this novel. In particular, I made use of the collections and am indebted to the staff and volunteers at The Grantham Historical Society, The Historical Society of Cheshire County, and The New Hampshire Historical Society. I had the opportunity to examine 18th and 19th century town meeting reports and minutes, pauper auction documents, diaries and account books, the school catalogue from the Fiske Seminary, and many other primary sources.

At the New Hampshire Historical Society in Concord, New Hampshire, Reference Librarian Paul Friday, and Director of Collections and Exhibits Wesley G. Balla were eager to share their deep knowledge of New Hampshire's past and recommend additional resources. I made use of online museum and library collections such as those at the Old Sturbridge Village Research Library. My past experiences working in education and interpretation at Historic Deerfield, Enfield Shaker Museum, and the John Hay Estate at The Fells allowed exploration into some fascinating periods in New Hampshire history.

I want to particularly acknowledge the Henry N. Flynt Library of Historic Deerfield and the Pocumtuck Valley Memorial Association (PVMA) Library, known collectively as the Memorial Libraries. Librarian Heather Harrington led me to account books of 18th century ciderists and other primary sources. She also took the time to read an early version of the manuscript and offer feedback. The libraries' collection of the *Dublin Seminar for New England Folklife Annual Proceedings Papers* are an invaluable source for research in New England regional history, vernacular culture, and historical archaeology.

During my time working at Historic Deerfield, I was the beneficiary of the deep knowledge of early New England generously shared by the corps of museum guides who interpret the collections and history of the village for visitors and scholars. Many of these guides are also practitioners of period trades and skills such as hearth cooking and spinning and weaving.

There were a number of competing agricultural almanac(k)s being published during this time period. *Pauper Auction* features epigraphs from *The New Hampshire, Maine and Vermont Almanac for the Year of our Lord, 1805. Containing more Astronomical Calculations than any Almanac of the size hitherto published in New England. With a variety of such matters and things as well, it is hoped, be useful and entertaining to the Reader. (Calculated for the Meridian of Gilmanton, N.H. – Lat: 43 °28' North. Long. 70° 54'West.)*

The choice of this particular almanac was due to the fact that the New Hampshire Lakes Region is the general setting for the book. Publisher Dudley Leavitt, of Gilmanton and Meredith, New Hampshire, was a polymath scientist, teacher, mathematician, writer, publisher, and farmer. His almanac was published from 1797-1896. Farmer's almanacs, such as *The Old Farmer's Almanac* (1792-present) are still published today.

For recipes (*receipts*) of the period, I consulted *The Art of Cookery Made Plain and Easy* (1747) by Hannah Glasse, and *American Cookery* (1796) by Amelia Simmons. For orchard management and cider-making in the period, I located *The American Orchardist; or, a Practical Treatise on the Culture and Management of Apple and Other Fruit Trees* (1822) by James Thatcher and *The Cider Makers' Hand Book - A Complete Guide for Making and Keeping Pure Cider* (1890) by J.M. Trowbridge. These books are still available as reprints.

For the use of Abenaki words in this book, I employed the text, *New Familiar Abenakis and English Dialogues* (1884) by Joseph Laurent, Abenakis Chief. For readers interested in learning more about Abenaki history and culture, I recommend *The Voice of the Dawn: An Autohistory of the Abenaki Nation* (2001) by Frederick Matthew Wiseman, and *The Western Abenakis of Vermont, 1600–1800: War, Migration, and the Survival of an Indian People* (1994) by Colin G. Calloway.

The book, *Firsting and Lasting: Writing Indians Out of Existence in New England* (2010) by Jean M. O'Brian reminded me that many of the local histories that sit on the shelves of New England historical societies and libraries consider "authentic" history starting at the arrival and progress of civilized European settlers. They include frequent assertions that the indigenous people in the region had ceased to exist.

There are two people I would like to acknowledge for their assistance in the use of the Abenaki language and advice on the Abenaki character in the story, Sozap Wzôkhilain, or Joseph Fisher. Anne Jennison, a storyteller, historian, educator, and artist with Abenaki heritage, reviewed an early draft of the novel and offered advice and corrections. She also produced a recording of the pronunciation of Abenaki vocabulary present in the story for use in the audiobook production. Jesse Bruchac is a traditional storyteller, musician, author, film consultant, and Abenaki language instructor. He graciously corrected Abenaki language errors. Both of these activist-educators are dedicated to retaining and sharing the culture, language, and arts of the Abenaki people.

In regards to meetinghouses, I drew inspiration from the work and advice of photo documentarian Paul Wainwright. He has published a book of large format images of the interiors and exteriors of New England meetinghouses entitled, *A Space for Faith: The Colonial Meetinghouses of New England* (2010) and maintains a website identifying existing meetinghouses across New England along with videos of his lectures on the subject.

For the town meetings that were held in these sacred/secular spaces, I appreciated *The New England Town Meeting: Democracy in Action* (1999) by Joseph F. Zimmerman. *Moved and Seconded: Town Meeting in New Hampshire, the Present, the Past, and the Future* (2012) by New Hampshire storyteller Rebecca Rule, provides a humorous look at the institution and the people who participate in this 250-year-old form of government in New England. Town meeting has been praised as being the most democratic form of rule, allowing all who participate to have their voices heard. Rebecca, a storyteller and author of numerous books about "Yankee" culture, was kind enough to review an early version of this book and offer support to the cause of sharing New England history and culture.

Today the town meeting still exists in parts of New England as a treasured heritage and participatory form of town government. It has evolved in a number of ways, most importantly including voting rights for all registered voters residing in the town, rather than the original franchise, open only to land-owning white men. The date is always the second Tuesday of March. Discussion is still contentious. The terms "warrant" and "article" are still used. Some town meetings still include a community dinner.

My own town historical society contains town meeting reports from the time period of the novel, documenting the bidding out of indigent town citizens. Of the town residents who attend the annual town meeting in contemporary times, few are aware of this former practice. I have attended town meeting in my town since I moved to New Hampshire from Massachusetts twenty five years ago. It has been quite an education.

Although I am surrounded by old farmhouses and walls, I turned to *Big House, Little House, Back House, Barn* (1984) by Thomas Hubka for insight into 19th century farm buildings. There is a pile (get it, rock pile) of books on New England stone walls. The two I reached for most often were *Sermons in Stone* by Susan Allport (1990) and *The Granite Kiss* by Kevin Gardner (2001). For a glimpse into everyday life inside a New England home during this period, I delved into *Our Own Snug Fireside* (1993) by Jane C. Nylander. *Bed Rugs* (2000) by Jessie Armstead Marshall is a rare examination of the embroidered bed rugs of the 18th and early 19th century. *Colonial New Hampshire* (2105) by Jere Daniell is a good place to start to pursue deeper knowledge of the history of this state during this time period.

The topic of pauper auctions, in particular, has been examined in scholarly research within the greater context of forms of social welfare across the history of the United

States. I began my inquiry with Benjamin Klebaner's classic 1955 treatise, *Pauper Auctions: The 'New England Method' of Public Poor Relief* and read academic articles as well as a number of New Hampshire town histories, town reports, and diaries. As the 1800s progressed, there was a gradual shift away from private housing of the poor toward institutionalizing the poor in almshouses or workhouses. This period is documented in *The Poorhouse: America's Forgotten Institution* (2005) by David Wagner.

My rural town library, Dunbar Free Library, cheerfully processed hundreds of my interlibrary loan requests, ranging from local histories to stone wall field guides. In particular, I would like to thank Dawn Huston, Terri Heepe, Joey Holmes, and Sandy Stephan-Strombom for their cheerful assistance. Over the past twenty years, my treasured Thursday Night Bookclub taught me to look at literature through a variety of diverse lenses. My husband John and son Shaun, have offered encouragement and have been good-humored recipients of random historical facts. Who doesn't want to hear about George Washington's secret smallpox vaccine campaign over dinner?

The talented and patient Mike Leister of Lighthouse Rocket Design created the memorable cover of *Pauper Auction* and assisted in developing the book layout.

I truly enjoyed working with author and editor Tim Horvath, who added encouragement and enthusiasm to copyediting and proofreading assistance. Sharon Comeau was an early reader, an honest critic, and a keen-eyed proofreader. I am indebted to my early readers Lisette Scott, Jackie Diebold, Janet Andrews, and Lindel Hart.

To try to walk in the shoes of the characters, I felt the responsibility to explore the world of craft cider making, which is experiencing an exciting resurgence across the United States. There are a number of old and new books on cider making and cider appreciation. *The American Cider Book: The Story of America's Natural Beverage* by Vrest Orton (1973) is written by the founder of the Vermont Country Store and includes recipes. An accessible how-to book is *Cider: Making, Using & Enjoying Sweet & Hard Cider* (2003) by Lew Nichols and Annie Proulx.

But to truly experience this historic and contemporary beverage, I recommend a New England road trip, particularly in my home state of New Hampshire, to explore craft ciderhouses and taprooms. Many orchards managed by agricultural preservationists are reintroducing heirloom apple varieties. For those who take the time to seek out these orchards and cideries, the reward is the opportunity to experience a regional heritage food and drink.

DISCUSSION QUESTIONS

1. This story takes place in a rural New Hampshire village in 1805, prior to the availability of state or federal security nets. What are your opinions about the definition used for "deserving poor" in Thorneboro? Is the pauper auction, as a form of public assistance, a cruelty or a kindness?

2. A pauper is generally considered one who requires alms or public monies, goods, or services. Paupers have little personal autonomy. Margery, Agnes, and Benjamin Meakin are paupers in Thorneboro, New Hampshire in 1805. Are there other ways to define "pauper" that would encompass other town residents?

3. Each character who lives on Wheeler Farm comes to find purpose and gratification in matching their creative gifts with their vocations. In particular, Agnes and Margery identify and develop their personal abilities to raise themselves from their status as paupers to empower themselves as scholar, artist, pupil, and teacher. What are the particular challenges of becoming an independent woman, in this time period?

4. There is a common American myth found in literature celebrating the self-reliance of rural farmers and settlers. How does the description of life in Thorneboro suggest the importance of mutual dependence?

5. Living in rural New Hampshire, despite its often-harsh climate, provides opportunity to live in the present moment among great natural beauty and resources. What are some of ways the Wheeler Farm residents take advantage of the natural world for nurturing, not just sustenance?

6. The author offers analogies and metaphors for human nature through description of craftwork such as blacksmithing, stone masonry, cidering, hearth cooking, and rug weaving. Does this enhance the understanding of the characters? How?

7. Orchards, apples, and food and drink made from apples are intertwined throughout the narrative. What specific apple-related symbolism did you notice?

8. One of the author's goals is to invoke an authentic sense of place. What descriptions help you to place yourself in the period and setting? How do the settings influence the characters or their actions?

9. Margery refers a number of times to "putting on her mask." One example is at Thanksgiving during her first year at Wheeler Farm. What are other examples of mask-wearing in the book? What are the purposes, benefits, or drawbacks of wearing masks?

10. Town meeting is an important part of the lives of Thorneboro residents. How does town meeting shape the lives of the residents? How do the residents shape town meeting? What are some of the spheres of power evident in this seemingly "democratic" institution? Have you experienced a town meeting? What are the benefits and drawbacks of the system?

11. Although Samuell and Joseph have the privilege of male gender at a time when women were denied many basic rights, the two men face challenges due to their sexual orientation. How are their lives and family relationships impacted in this time period when homosexuality is both a civil criminal offense and a sin in the eyes of the Christian church? What do you imagine the future holds for the two men?

12. Joseph faces additional discrimination and displacement due to his Abenaki ethnicity. How is he able to retain his identity, beliefs, and values as he lives among those who have stolen First Nation land?

13. Samuell's mother and Joseph's mother both love their sons without reserve, but make different choices in how to best protect their children. What do you think of their mothers' actions?

14. What events or actions contribute most significantly to the familial feelings that develop between the individuals living on Wheeler Farm? Can this group living under one roof be called a family?

15. Why do you think Meakin defies his sponsor and steps up to help with the apple harvest after Samuell's injury? How does this balance against his previous irresponsible behavior? As he leaves the village to try to restore his family, do you think he will be able to maintain his reformed goals?

16. What are your thoughts about the murder of Jacob Kimball? Do you think there is ever justification for the use of defensive or deadly force in the face of a threat of death or grievous harm?

17. What do you think explains Agnes's passion for languages? What do you envision for her future?

18. Are there any other topics from the book that you would like to discuss?

ABOUT THE AUTHOR

Mary Kronenwetter is by birth and disposition a New Englander and grew up in a 19th century Massachusetts farmhouse complete with barn and outbuildings, well, and stone wall-lined pasture and fields. She holds a doctorate in education and has taught at colleges in the United States, China, and Japan. Mary lives in the Dartmouth-Lake Sunapee Region of New Hampshire and has served as a museum educator at Historic Deerfield, The John Hay Estate at The Fells and the Enfield Shaker Museum.

To contact Mary or learn more about New Hampshire's rural past and explore the historical places and practices that informed the creation of *Pauper Auction*, please visit the website *marykronenwetter.com* or her bookstagram at *instagram.com/marykronenwetterauthor/*.

Please consider supporting your local independent bookstore.

*Reviews of **Pauper Auction** on your chosen retailer's website are greatly appreciated.*

www.ingramcontent.com/pod-product-compliance
Lightning Source LLC
Chambersburg PA
CBHW032017150726
47990CB00005B/2004